Snodgrass and Harper
Detective Agency

Snodgrass and Harper Detective Agency

The Doctor is Not In

A.M. Overett

The Snodgrass and Harper Detective Agency

The Doctor is Not In

Published by
Lighthouse Publishing
SAN 257-4330
228 Freedom Parkway
Hoschton, GA 30548
United States of America

www.lighthousechristianpublishing.com

TABLE OF CONTENTS:

CHAPTER 1
Origins of a Detective Agency

Donovan "Don" Snodgrass and Henri Harper had worked in the washing machine business for many years. Donovan as a repairman and Henri as an actual washer of dishes. When their paths crossed twenty years earlier it was "bros" at first sight. How did their friendship thrive? Well, many things; a love of beer, pool halls, football, motorcycles, ambient music, and ancient Chinese art.

It was Donovan who, while tiring of his career, invited Henri to join him in the detective agency he was starting. Henri jumped at the chance having also tired of washing dishes. He also liked to jump. So with enthusiasm, energy, and lower-than-average IQs, the Snodgrass and Harper Detective Agency was born. They borrowed a few thousand from a local bank and began to set up shop in a strip mall just across the street from the Police Department. They thought being around law enforcement would lend itself to giving them cases. Let's look at this dynamic duo as they begin their first day on the job...

"Okay Henri, we need to come up with a good slogan for our sign outside. What do you think?"

"How about this - 'Good detectives at a good rate.'?"

"Nah, not eye-grabbing enough. You know, when I was a repairman, I was once called 'incompetent'. The man was smiling so I think it was a compliment."

"Is that good?"

"Sure, it is. Anything with 'in' in the word is good, you know like inside is better than outside?"

"Oh okay, like inward..."

"Incarcerated, inept..."

"We also need to speak about our experience."

"But we don't have any."

"Well, we've been thinking about this idea for a year and a half."

"Yeah, but thinking about something rather than doing something is something different altogether."

"I know but we got to start somewhere. Let's see. I've thought about it for a year and a half, and you have thought about it for a year and a half so that's three years. So how about this..."Incompetent for 3 years."?

And so, the boy's new slogan was born. They printed up signs and business cards and were on their way to new heights.

The following day, they had their first client. Dr. Celia Delworth wanted to employ the boys to follow her husband whom she suspected was cheating on her with another woman.

"So, Dr. Delworth. How did you hear about our firm? Was it the catchy sign outside?"

"Ah, not really. I was speaking with a police officer outside and he pointed to your office. He said if you want top-rate service, you should see the chumps over there. I think he meant champs, so I came over."

"Okay, and why do you think your husband is having an affair?"

"Well, he comes home smelling of perfume. He typically comes home after 1 a.m. He never used to do that at the beginning of our marriage."

"Can I get you something Dr. Delworth…you look a bit rattled?"

"Oh, I'm sorry. It's just my best friend just passed away."

"Oh, I'm sorry to hear that. What happened to her?"

"She died in a terrible umbrella accident. It was so unexpected. And it wasn't even raining that day."

"Oh, I'm sorry to hear that. Can you give me a description of your husband?

"Yes, he's 6' 1" tall, very handsome. Brown hair with bright blue eyes. Strong chin, and very chiseled features. Very muscular. Works out daily."

"Any distinguishing features, tattoos, etc."

"He has the ability to fly and has x-ray vision."

"Excuse me? That sounds a lot like Super Man."

"Yes, it is."

"Well, Superman doesn't exist."

"Yes, sad, isn't it?"

"So, your husband…doesn't exist?"

"Correct. I just made him up. My mother has been pushing me to get a husband for the last ten years, so I pretended to be married."

"Okay, so there isn't a case?"

"Oh yes there is, and I will pay you for it. I just need you to pretend to be following my husband."

"But if he doesn't exist, how can we follow him?"

"I just want you to look like you are following him. You see, my mother is a very persistent person. When she said she wanted to meet my husband I told her we were having marital difficulties. She thinks that we have separated and that he is living somewhere else."

"Ok, I'm still a little fuzzy."

"I want you to come over when my mother is there and explain your findings."

"And what findings are those?"

"That my husband is having an affair."

"You mean that your imaginary husband is having an affair?"

"Yes, my imaginary husband is having an imaginary affair."

"Okay, so just show up at your house and make up stuff?"

"Well, I would like it to be as real as possible. Maybe you could take some photos or something?"

"Photos of what?"

"My imaginary husband."

"Oh, okay. So try and find some people that look like your fake husband and take pictures of them?"

"Precisely."

Just then Henri Harper walks in. He takes the woman's hand and softly kisses it.

"Asante mademoiselle. And what is your name?"

"Oh, Dr. Delworth, this is my partner, Henri Harper. Henri, this is Dr. Gloria Delworth."

"Very nice to meet you Dr. Delworth. You know you are the spitting image of Gloria Swanson?"

"Oh, really? Why thank you. My first name is Celia by the way."

"Not the Gloria Swanson from 1941 but more the Gloria Swanson from 1981."

"Oh really?"

"You know the period where she was not so famous and was putting on weight?"

"Ok thanks Henri," Snodgrass said waving his hand trying to get Harper to stop.

"You know when she retired to the South of France and was really putting on the pounds."

"Ok enough Harper…"

"But your face is gorgeous just like hers in 1958."

At that point, Dr. Delworth just began to nod her head knowing she was dealing with someone who was a little off.

"Your face, though slightly asymmetrical, is exactly the same. Could you turn your head slightly like this?" Harper moves his head slightly to the side and points to Dr. Delworth to do the same.

"Look Harper, Dr. Delworth doesn't need to tilt her head in some odd way. Let's just move on Dr. Delworth…"

In some odd editing effect, Harper reappears from another room with a step ladder. He wants to be able to peer down on Dr. Delworth to confirm that she does have a similar look to Gloria Swanson if viewed from a slightly higher angle. Snodgrass puts an immediate stop to this line of inquiry by kicking the step ladder from underneath Harper causing Harper to land in a crumpled heap.

"And how can we help you today Dr. Delwoth?" Harper extended his hand to shake while still on the floor.

"Dr. Delworth is employing us to surveil her husband…who doesn't exist."

"I'm sorry, what are we doing?"

For the next twenty minutes, Snodgrass tried to explain to Harper what they had been employed to do by Dr. Delworth. It sort of sank in but ultimately Harper didn't have a clue.

Just then an elderly gentleman walks in.

"Hello, is this the travel agency?"

"No sir we're a detective agency."

"Oh, I see. My eyesight and hearing are not so good. Can I buy a ticket to London?"

"No sir. I don't think you understand, we're a detective agency and not a travel agency."

"Look, I came all the way over here on the number 13 bus and I demand a little service."

Harper nodded to Snodgrass and escorted the gentleman over to his desk.

"Okay Dr. Delworth, let me work on the pictures and we'll meet tomorrow afternoon, how does that sound?"

"That would be great. And here is a check for the first part of your services."

Snodgrass was dumbfounded to receive a check for 2,000 dollars. They hadn't done anything yet and they already had two grand. He tried to hide his giddiness as he knew it would not look professional.

"Okay Dr. Delmonte, we'll get right on it."

"That's Delworth."

"Oh, yes, sorry, what did I say?"

"Dr. Delmonte."

"Oh Delmonte, like the food company."

"I guess, anyway, come over to my place at 4 pm tomorrow afternoon and we'll go over whatever you have. My mother will also be there."

"Okay, sounds good."

Snodgrass began to smile as he looked over the check. Just then he noticed the elderly gentleman walking out with a big smile on his face.

"What did you tell him Harper?"

"Oh, I booked him a ticket to London on one of the travel websites."

"Oh, that was clever of you Harper."

"Why thank you, Donavan."

A few minutes later Dominic Rizzo walks into the office.

"Heyah wheres-ah the rento?"

Dominic Rizzo is the owner of the building where Snodgrass and Harper have their agency. Although a 4th generation Italian born in Indiana, he has an MBA from Ohio State, but likes to pretend to Snodgrass and Harper that he's in the mafia so they will pay their rent on time.

"You know, if I don't-ah get the rento...well...batta bing batta boom."

"Ah no Mr. Rizzo we have the rent money right here. We just got paid for a first job."

"Fantastico! No batta bing batta boom for you. No bipitty boppity boo."

"Isn't that from Cinderella?"

"Cinderella, what kind of macho Italiano mafioso do you think I am?"

Harper and Snodgrass just shrugged their shoulders.

"Look Mr. Rizzo. I'll go down to the bank today and get your money. You'll have it first thing in the morning."

Mr. Rizzo began to shake his head but kept a keen eye on the two. He had a toothpick in his mouth that he liked to twirl around for effect, but it was mostly a prop.

CHAPTER 2
Surveillance

The following morning, Harper had a dentist appointment. Snodgrass accompanied him to provide support and "other things."

"Good morning Mr. Harper, the dentist will see you now," said a blonde, leggy receptionist at the front desk. The receptionist known as "Mercury," was a Russian spy, who was trying to find secret information about the American Dental Association, as well as find her long lost "Babushka," who came over from the "old country" twenty years earlier.

"Hello, and how are you today Mr. Harper?" asked Dr. Phillip P. Greenlawn. The P was for Perspicacious. He had weird parents.

"I am doing okay, how about you?"

"Great, why don't we get started? If you would please take the chair."

"Take it where?"

Snodgrass pointed to the reclining dental chair.

"Oh, yes, of course."

"Please make yourself comfortable."

Just then, another tall, blonde, leggy woman walked into the room. She also happened to be a Russian spy who was surveilling the barber shop next door that had been set up by an ex-KGB operative who had fled the old Soviet Union.

"Gentlemen, this is Miss Svetlana Melanoma."

"How do you do gentlemen?" she said in a low sexy voice.

The boys returned her greeting, and the dentist was soon at work on Harper's tooth. He had been complaining about a toothache he had had for the past several weeks. The complaining had done little good as there was no one there to listen to it.

"Well, Mr. Harper I can see this tooth will need to be extracted."

"Extracted where?"

"Out of your mouth Harper."

"Oh no, really?"

"Yes, unfortunately."

"If you like I can take it out now for you."

Harper began to think, which was never a good idea.

"It's best just to get it over with Harper," said Snodgrass.

"Ok, doctor let's do it. Are you going to give me amnesia?

"You mean anesthesia?"

"I thought it was amnesia. You know to make you forget about the pain?"

"Well, amnesia is where you just forget about things, anesthesia numbs the gum, so you don't feel the pain."

"But wouldn't it be better if I just forgot about it?"

"You mean after the fact? Wouldn't be better to numb the tooth so you don't feel the pain in the first place?"

"I guess it's one of those space-time continuum thingys."

"Yes, I guess so. So open your mouth and we'll get started."

Harper complied with the dentist's request and opened his mouth. The dentist then raised a large syringe that had the Novocain.

"What is that?!!!" Harper screamed, practically jumping out of the chair.

"Calm down Mr. Harper, it's just a little shot to help numb your tooth."

"A little shot, that's a great big shot! Are you sure you can't just give me amnesia?"

At that point, Snodgrass hauled off and slugged Harper in the face, sending him back in the chair.

"There you go, Harper. Now you have amnesia," Snodgrass said. Go ahead doc."

As the dentist applied the normal anesthesia, Snodgrass began to look around the office and noticed a Soviet theme to the décor and artwork. There was even an Andy Warhol-inspired depiction of Joseph Stalin similar to the one he did on Marilyn Monroe. Was the dentist's office some sort of front for Russian intelligence?

Once the dentist had finished removing Harper's tooth, Snodgrass slowly dragged Harper out of the office and down to the car.

Later that night, the boys went looking for a fake Mr. Delworth.

"Okay Don, what are we doing again?"

"Uh well, we're on a stakeout. I've got my oPhone set up to take a video of that house over there."

"Whose house, is it?"

"I don't know."

"You don't know? Then why are we here?"

"I told you. We are supposed to fake a stakeout and take video or pictures of Dr. Delworth's husband."

"I thought she didn't have a husband?"

"She doesn't."

"Then why are we here?"

"There's a guy who has an office in the same building as we do. He lives here and has a wife. We will take pictures of him when they go and pretend its Dr. Delworth's husband cheating on Dr. Delworth."

"How do you know about this guy?"

"Mr. Rizzo told me about him. By the way, Mr. Rizzo is in the backseat."

"Hiyuh fellas!!!!"

Harper's heart practically leapt out of his chest when Mr. Rizzo popped up from the backseat.

"Mr. Rizzo, what are you doing here?"

"Don said I could join you. Oh, and please call me Dom."

Harper mulled over the fact that there was a "Don" and a "Dom." What if Don became a Mafia Don he wondered to himself.

"Okay Dom, but…wait a minute. What happened to your Italian accent."

"Funny story, I don't have one. I just use it on people when I am trying to collect the rent."

"Wow, very effective."

"Anyway, Don was asking me if I knew any couples that he could surveil. I said sure if he would let me hang out with you guys for the stakeout."

"Well, it's not really a stakeout per se. We just need some fake photos."

"Oh yeah, forgot. Anyway, these are the Phillips, Brad, and Hailey. Brad has an insurance business on the first floor. Brad told me that he and Hailey go out every Thursday at 8 pm. It's like their date night. Anyway, when I heard of your predicament, I immediately thought that the Phillips could be your fake cheating couple."

Just as Dom said, the couple left the house for the evening. Don took video and some still shots. With their mission complete, they headed home. Actually, they stopped for a burrito at a local burrito stand; Tito's Burritos before heading home.

The following day, Snodgrass and Harper arrived at Dr. Delworth's home at 4 pm. The home was in a fancy part of town called Del-Air. It was a gated community with an Olympic size pool, rec center and fitness room. Dr. Delworth had a beautiful five-bedroom home that had the feel of a villa in Tuscany.

"Wow, nice place you have here Dr. Delworth. By the way, since you are not married, should we be calling you 'Dr. Delworth?'"

Dr. Delworth was confused by Harper's question. "I'm not sure what you mean. I am a doctor."

"Isn't there a married version of doctor, like Mrs. Doctor?"

"Dr. Delworth is fine."

"Never mind him, doctor, he just had a tooth extracted…apparently along with part of his brain."

"Okay, let's see the pictures."

Snodgrass handed Dr. Delworth the pictures and she began to examine them.

"No, no, these will not do!"

"Why, I thought the couple in the pictures could be used as your cheating husband and his mistress?"

"No but look. He looks too innocent to be a cheating husband."

"What does a cheating husband look like?"

"You know kind of shifty, someone who thinks he's being followed."

"Okay, so we need to follow someone and make them think they are being followed so they look suspicious?"

"Exactly."

"Hey, couldn't we just go online and find someone who looks shifty and use their photos?"

"No, because we also need some video."

"Maybe there's some online video."

"Well, however you do it is fine by me, just do it. I've paid you good money and we need to find the perfect cheating husband to fool my mother."

"Isn't she supposed to be here?"

"No, she's not coming over until 6 pm. I didn't tell her you were coming over tonight in case there were issues with the photos. So go find a better subject and get back to me as soon as you can. I can't keep stalling my mother."

"Okay, we're on our way!" Snodgrass shouted unsure how they were supposed to locate this "shifty" individual who didn't exist.

"Hey, I have a good idea," Harper barked as the pair got into their car. "Why don't we get Rizzo to be shifty cheating husband?"

"Hey Harper, that might work. Let's go over to the office and check with him."

When they arrived at the office, they found Rizzo trying to get the rent from one of the tenants.

"Hey-ah, you needah to pay the rento pronto Mizzas Peabody."

Mrs. Peabody was a kindly older lady who ran a hair salon in the building."

"Mr. Rizzo, it's been a slow month. Can you give me until the 15th?"

"Hey-ah, whatdya think I run here-ah, a charity? I needah the rentah nowah."

Harper and Snodgrass thought that Rizzo was being a little too harsh with Mrs. Peabody. As they studied Rizzo, they realized just how bad his Italian accent was. It was mostly the hand gestures that he used that were meant to convey his Mediterranean motif. He also wore a leisure suit from the 70s that had a dress shirt unbuttoned down to his stomach revealing a rather hairy chest that the boys wondered if it was fake hair glued on.

"I tells you what Mizzas ah Peobody-ah. You betta have that-ah rento to me by the 15th-ah or I get Rocco and Giuseppe to pay that-ah lovely daughter of yours a visit. Capish?"

"Yes, yes, Mr. Rizzo, I will have it to you on the 15th."

A rather horrified Mrs. Peabody left the building as fast as she could.

"Coming on a little strong there didn't you Dom?"

"No, not really. She always pays late."

"Who are Rocco and Giuseppe?"

"Oh, they're my dogs," he said with a bright smile. "So where do we stand with the investigation? Did you talk with Dr. Delworth?"

"Yeah, but unfortunately she didn't like the photos."

"What's not to like?"

"She said the subject wasn't shifty enough."

"Shifty?"

"Yeah, you know, like someone who is acting suspicious. Speaking of which, could we use you for the photos?"

"Sure, why not?"

CHAPTER 3
A New Suspect

For the next couple of hours, the boys had Rizzo walking down the street acting as shifty as he could. They tried to find out-of-the-way places, but people kept walking by, many of them with puzzled expressions on their faces. The boys finally got what they thought they needed and then called Dr. Delworth. They arranged to meet her the next day.

The following day they presented the new pictures to Dr. Delworth.

"No, no these will not do. I guess I'll have to help you. Let's get in the car and I will find someone suitable."

The boys shrugged their shoulders and were soon driving off in Dr. Delworth's Mercedes. They noticed quickly that Dr. Delworth seemed to be driving to a particular location. It didn't appear she was looking for random people. They parked downtown on Main Street near the Parkside Bistro. The Parkside Bistro was a fancy shop where a lot of the town's movers and shakers would often take lunch or grab a coffee often appearing to move or shake.

The trio ran inside the coffee shop and began to make their orders. Dr. Delworth made hers...

"I'd like a triple mocha latte with half-caf half decaf, a sprinkle of cinnamon, a dash of apple cider, a teaspoon of goat's milk one granule of Indian pure cane sugar, no whip, a caramel drizzle, and a swizzle stick."

"Two black coffees for us," Snodgrass said pointing to himself and Harper.

Once their orders were made, they found a table by the rear of the shop. This allowed for a view of the entire establishment. The boys began to look around for a potential fake Mr. Delworth.

"I have to say Dr. Delworth you look lovely today," Harper said. She was sporting a floral pattern dress with a matching scarf and large-lens sunglasses.

"You look like a middle-aged Debby Reynolds. You now maybe 35 to 38 years old."

"Oh, thank you."

"You know right before her career tanked and she started gaining a few pounds..."

"...Harper here is a bit of a movie buff."

"Oh really, have you ever thought about acting?" Dr. Delworth queried.

"As a matter of fact, I am one of the main players at the Whisby Theatre Company."

"I wouldn't say 'main' players but Harper is working on it. A potential Sir Alec Baldwin."

"I think that's Sir Alec Guinness."

"Okay, I may not be the main player but I'm working on it. I'm taking lessons on the side."

"I have a few friends in the business. Maybe I could get you an audition?" Dr. Delworth suggested. Like a hungry pup, Harper nodded his head. All that was missing was his upraised hands bent and his tongue wagging back and forth.

"I don't think there is much to acting. You just need to use your imagination." Snodgrass pondered.

Harper put his index finger to his lip and began to imagine himself as a movie star. He imagined being a handsome and debonair actor from the thirties, on set in a remake of the Curse of the Mummy. He could see the pyramids and the Nile.

"Harper, Harper, snap out of it!" Snodgrass said as he began to snap his fingers in Harper's face.

"Look over there boys by the window, that's the guy I want."

Toward the front of the coffee shop, sitting by himself at a table and looking intently at his laptop was a rather young and extremely handsome man. Snodgrass and Harper thought that maybe she was flattering herself a little too much thinking that this man could be her husband. He must have been 10-15 years younger than her."

"I want you to get some video/pictures of that man."

"Okay, will do. Now, what if he doesn't have a girlfriend?"

"No problem, you can photoshop one in."

"Isn't that what I said earlier? We could just pull something off the internet for both the fake husband and the fake girlfriend he is using to cheat you with, on, whatever."

"No, it has to be a very specific man otherwise my mother will see through the ruse."

"Okay, will do, but we'll need more money."

"More money? I already paid you two grand."

"Yes, but we already put in more than two grand worth of hours."

"Very well, I'll get you the money when you get me the photo."

The next day the boys began to monitor the movements of the new fake Mr. Delworth. They wanted to see if they could get him into a location where they could take some pictures. He seemed to be at the coffee shop a lot and for most of the day. They decided they would just take some photos of him from the car and as suggested by Dr. Delworth photoshop in some other girl.

"We still need some video though. How long is this going to take?"

"I don't know, he seems to live at this place."

The boys waited another several hours before the fake Mr. Delworth packed up his laptop and headed out. They followed him down the street for several blocks before he turned into a large brick building. It appeared to be an older building from the turn of the century. It was a dark gothic-looking building. The boys couldn't tell for what purpose it was; commercial or maybe residential.

As the boys entered, they were greeted by a receptionist who was behind a translucent and modern-looking clear desk. Its appearance was in complete juxtaposition with the exterior of the building.

"Good afternoon gentlemen, how can I help you?"

"Did you see a man just walk into the building miss?"

"I've seen lots of men. Anyone, in particular, you are looking for?"

"Well, he's about 6' 3". Dark brown hair, very good looking. He was wearing a dress shirt and had a black overcoat on…very stylish."

"Well, we have a lot of those here. This is the Hyde Building. It's for the up-and-coming executive type. We lease office space on floors 4 through 12 and floors 12 through 25 are executive office suites. Floors 26 through 50 are residential – luxury condominiums typically owned by the professionals who use the office spaces below them."

"Interesting. So, the description we gave could be any number of people?"

"Yes. Do you have a picture?"

"Sorry, we don't…"

"Let me try to describe him to her," Harper pushed his way forward.

"Ma'am…sorry what's your name?"

"Elizabeth.'

"Elizabeth, what a beautiful name. Just like the owner of it."

"Why thank you."

"You know Elizabeth Taylor looked like you at your age. How old are you?"

"Oh, I'm twenty-four."

"Yes, you almost look like her when she was twenty-four that is to say you remind me of her at twenty-four. I don't mean when I was twenty-four, I mean that when you were twenty-four, which is now, you reminded me of her when she was twenty-four…"

"Okay, we get it Harper, can you describe the man we are looking for to Elizabeth?"

"Oh, yes, sorry…by the way you also look a little like Elizabeth Montgomery…"

"Get on with it!" snapped a rather agitated Snodgrass.

"Do you have a paper and pencil Ms. Elizabeth?"

"Oh yes, right here."

"Thank you." Harper proceeded to begin sketching what he thought looked like the man they were following. He was working diligently at it often squinting his eyes and pursing his lips as a means of trying to extract the various facial features of the subject. When he had concluded he showed it to Elizabeth.

"Look familiar?"

Snodgrass peered over the sketch and immediately began to roll his eyes.

"How in the world is she going to be able to identify the man from that mess?"

"Mess? I'll have you know I took many an art class in high school."

"Yes, but this looks like a stick figure with a triton sticking out of his head."

"That triton as you call it is actually his wonderful flowing dark brown locks of hair."

"Elizabeth, I am sorry we wasted your time," Snodgrass said as he ushered Harper out of the front lobby.

"So, what do we do now? We have been charged by Dr. Delworth to take pictures of a guy who is somewhere in a fifty-story building."

"Let's go over to her house and explain."

"Can't you just call her?"

"Well, I want to see about getting that additional two grand."

Harper nodded his head and the two proceeded to Dr. Delworth's house, along with the persuasive Mr. Rizzo.

CHAPTER 4
A Trip to (in) the Park

When the trio arrived at Dr. Delworth's house they had to be buzzed in at the front gate.

"Hi Dr. Delworth, it's me, Donavan Snodgrass and Henri Harper. Can we come in and speak with you for a minute about the case?"

"Can't you just call?"

"Well, we have something to show you."

"Really, what? Can't you just text or email it to me?"

"It would just be better if we could come in and speak with you."

"Alright."

The gate buzzed and then began to swing open. The trio drove through and began to go down the main street toward Dr. Delworth's house. The neighborhood was decked out in Christmas Lights as well as various nativity scenes and related seasonal displays. The boys began to reminisce about their childhoods.

"I remember my dad getting up on the ladder on the outside of our house and stringing up lights," Snodgrass said fondly.

"Yeah, I remember making snowmen and playing in the snow with my brother and sister and then coming and having hot cocoa by the fireplace," Harper said in a dreamy voice.

"All I remember was my dad throwing baseballs at me."

"Oh, he would give you batting practice?"

"No, he would just randomly throw baseballs at me."

Snodgrass and Harper had looks of concern as they listened to Rizzo reliving his childhood.

As they arrived at Dr. Delworth's house, they sprang out of the car and ran to the front door. They rang the doorbell and Dr. Delworth appeared in a festive red dress.

"Come in boys."

As she realized there were three of them she questioned Rizzo's presence.

"And who is this?"

"Hello-ah, Dr. Delworth-ah. I'ma, the boys-ah beesness manager-ah, Mista Rizzo."

"Oh, ah nice to meet you Mr. Rizzo. Can I get anyone a drink or something?"

"I'll have a spritzer if you have it?" Harper asked.

"A spritzer?" Dr. Delworth asked with a puzzled look on her face.

"Really Harper, you want a spritzer."

"I mean she's asking."

"No, no that's fine. How would you like it?"

"Well if you have some Chardonnay and some grapefruit mineral water that would be perfect."

Rizzo and Snodgrass rolled their eyes wondering how Harper would want something like that.

"Um, let me go look. Why don't you all make yourselves at home while I look."

Rizzo and Snodgrass took a seat on a nearby couch while Harper followed Dr. Delworth into the kitchen. Soon after, she popped her head from behind the kitchen door and asked Rizzo and Snodgrass if they wanted anything."

"I guess I'll have a beer if you have one," Snodgrass asked.

"I'll have a spumante if you have it."

Snodgrass gave Rizzo a look like *you too.*

"Hey, I thought you were supposed to play the heavy?"

"I can't have a spumante and look intimidating at the same time?"

"No!!!"

"Everything okay out there?"

"Yes, Dr. Delworth!" both Rizzo and Snodgrass replied simultaneously.

A few minutes later Dr. Delworth returned from the kitchen with a tray of drinks. Harper was in tow with his spritzer in hand.

"So, you see Dr. Delworth that is why *My Life as Dog* was really an allegory for why we are really living a dog's life."

"Oh, I see," a confused Dr. Delworth said to Harper.

"Ah Dr. Delworth-ah, I need-ah to ask-ah..." before Rizzo could finish what he was about to say the doorbell rang. Dr. Delworth ran up to the door and looked through the peephole.

"Oh no, it's my mother! You'll need to get out of here. Go out the back door!"

"But what about the spitzer?"

"Never mind knucklehead, let's move!"

As the men were leaving out the back, they noticed an ominous-looking stairwell that led to the basement. They wondered if it was her home office. Whatever it was it looked uninviting.

The next day, the boys managed to follow the fake Mr. Delworth into the second floor of the main office buildings. They saw him go into a large conference room and quickly did the same. Inside there must have been about fifty people seated. Toward the front was a podium and a gentleman with thick-rimmed glasses and a balding head beginning to speak.

"Thank you for coming today. I would like to speak to you about how *Today's Office Place Should Look and Feel*," the man opened as the boys found a couple of chairs toward the back of the room. The gentleman looked distinctly out of place with a very old brown suit and tie that looked like something an executive would have worn during the sixties. Snodgrass surveyed the room and could see the fake Mr. Delworth in the front row.

"Hello everyone, I am Mr. Clydesdale, like the horse. What does today's workplace look like today you ask? Well, it looks like gray floors, gray walls, and acoustic tiling on the ceiling." Everyone was quiet waiting for the man to continue.

"Just kidding," he said in a very dry tone that took everyone by surprise.

"Yes, today's workplace will look different. It will be diverse; many different ethnic backgrounds, and different beliefs and made up of both men and women. It will take everyone's opinions and mix them up into a great big pot of gumbo that we can all enjoy. Yum, yum." The boys looked over to the fake Mr. Delworth who looked completely bored with the presentation.

"Today's workplace is like a Saturn B5 rocket going into outer space. It is long, tubular, and very powerful. And there is plenty of Tang if you get my meaning, he, he, he, ha, ha, ha…"

At that point, the fake Mr. Delworth got up and left the meeting and the boys got up to follow him.

"If you turn in your outlines to page 10 you will get a good idea of what the modern workplace will be like. It is full of orangutans and lots of bananas. Oops, sorry wrong page. That's a picture of our Malaysia office."

The fake Mr. Delworth went through the door leading to the emergency stairwell. The boys in hot pursuit went through the same door but could not detect which direction he went.

"I'll go up and you go down. See what you can find."

Harper nodded and immediately began to descend the stairs. When he reached the bottom he saw the exit door was slightly ajar and ran over to check it. It opened to the street and he quickly ran outside to see if he could spot the fake Mr. Delworth. Meanwhile, Snodgrass ran up to the top floor and ran up to the roof. Once on top, there was no one there. He then called Harper on his cell phone.

"Harper, any luck?"

"No, nothing."

"Okay, he's given us the slip. Let's head over to the office."

"I can't, I have theatre rehearsal tonight."

"Tonight? Oh, okay. Well, let's get an early start tomorrow.

Harper, who enjoyed amateur theatrics, was also secretly wanting to become a Hollywood star. By some miracle, he had managed to earn a role in a production of

Shakespeare's *A Midsummer Night's Dream* as Tom Snout.

To Harper's surprise, right before one of the rehearsals, the director introduced a new member of the cast.

"Everyone, if you will gather around, please. Unfortunately, we lost another one of our players. Larry Finklebaum, our terrific Bottom has been in an accident. Some sort of incident involving an umbrella. Anyway, I'd like to introduce to you William "Billy" Friendwich."

The rest of the cast gave Billy a round of low-key applause but Harper was stunned. "Billy," was Dr. Delworth's fake husband. Had she employed an actor to fulfill the role of her missing husband? The plot was thickening, both on stage and in real life. For the rest of the evening, Harper kept close tabs on "Billy."

After rehearsal, he ran over to Snodgrass's apartment to let him know what was going on.

"Don, you won't believe who I saw tonight?"

"Who?"

"Dr. Delworth's fake husband."

"Really, where?"

"He was at the rehearsal. He's a part of the cast. Larry Finklebaum had to drop out due to an umbrella accident."

"Wow, and what's his name."

"William…" Harper raised his hands and made quotation marks with his fingers. "'Billy' Friendwich."

"Why are you doing that?"

"Doing what?"

"Making quotation marks in the air?"

"Well he was introduced as William "Billy" Friendwich."

"And?"

"So when you are introduced with your full first name and then a nickname, don't you need to make quotation marks in the air?"

"No, you can just say William "Billy" Friendwich, or you can just say Billy Friendwich."

"But won't that be confusing?" Harper then raises his hand and makes a gesture of a squiggly line in the air.

"Now what are you doing?"

"I'm making a question mark."

"You don't have to use your hands every time you want to use punctuation marks."

"Oh, okay."

Harper looked sad when he found out he didn't need to express every punctuation mark with his hands.

Just then Dominic Rizzo walked in with another gentleman.

"Hey guys, what's going on?"

"Well, we just found out that the guy who is the fake Mr. Delworth is in Harper's drama troupe."

"Troupe ?" Harper questioned the term.

"Yes, drama troupe."

"Troupe, I thought of it more of a drama club."

"Troupe, club, whatever."

"Well, Troupe is more related to dramatists who have a traveling show." The mystery gentleman stated.

"Who is this?" Snodgrass asked Rizzo.

"Oh, this is Lars Olafsson. He's a friend of mine from Denmark."

"How do you do Lars? I'm Donovan Snodgrass and this is my associate Henri Harper."

"Please to meet you both," Lars extended his hand to shake.

"What do you do for a living Lars?"

"I'm a path-maker for the local parks and recreation department."

"Really, what does that involve?" Asked Snodgrass.

"I design all the paths and trails through the various parks."

"Wow, that sounds interesting. You're like a trailblazer so to speak," Harper said.

"Yes, it's a very specialized skill creating these hiking paths. People nowadays expect to have a special experience when they are out walking. They work hard all week and they want to get an experience that will be relaxing and make them feel they are back to nature. So it's my job to create an "experience" so to speak," Lars said putting up his two fingers on both hands and making air quotes.

"See Don, Lars is doing the air quotes."

"Never mind Harper. Anyway, it's good to meet you Lars. Dominic, we need to go find this "Mr. Delworth" character and find out what's going on."

Everyone watched Snodgrass to see if he would make air quotes. When he didn't they all just continued with the task at hand.

After the rehearsal the following evening, Snodgrass, Harper, Dominic, and Lars, went to the playhouse to speak to "Mr. Delworth."

"Hey Skip, do you know where Billy is tonight?" Skip was the stage manager. He had worked at the Whisby Playhouse for over thirty years as a stage manager. To say he was crusty was an understatement.

When he would move, little pieces of crust would break off.

"I haven't seen him, Henri. He did mention that he and his wife were going to take a walk in the park tonight."

"But didn't he need to rehearse that scene with the maiden in the third act?"

"No, he already nailed it the other night. The director said he was good to go."

"What, I have had to rehearse my scenes over and over."

"Yes, that's because you are a bad actor."

"Bad actor? Bad actor?"

"Yes, you are a bad actor."

"Well, didn't director Steve tell me the other day that I had great subtext when reading my parts?"

"He said you had a great Rolex...you know on your wrist."

"Now why would he say that?"

"Because he couldn't think about anything else nice to say about you."

"Okay, never mind Harper. Skip, what park are the Delworth's going to?"

"It must be the Whisby Park down the street."

"Okay, thanks, let's go guys.

The boys then ran down the street to see if they could find the Delworths.

"Boy, it sure is dark in there. How are we going to find them?" asked Harper.

"Lars, didn't you design the layout of this park?" Dominic asked.

"Yes, Dominic I did. I know it like the back of my hand."

"Excellent, then you lead the way."

"Okay, let's go."

The entrance to the park where the boys entered was poorly lit so it required the expertise of Lars to get them to the better-lit areas of the park. Lars seemed to weave his way in and out of various trails and paths through the park. The boys frantically tried to keep up with his pace but it was difficult.

As they maneuvered toward the main path where most people would be Lars forgot to mention that there was a sign that marked the start of the hiking trail. The sign, supported by two large posts, was a 2-foot by 9-foot wooden banner that spelled out "Whisby Park Hiking Trail." The problem was that the sign had been installed over fifty years earlier and did not have cement anchors so the two posts bearing the sign had slowly descended into the wet ground where the hiking trail began. The further problem with that was that now the sign was only five feet above the ground and not the original eleven feet it had been when the sign was first constructed. Before he remembered to tell everyone to duck, Harper plowed into the sign sending him careening backward. Unaware of what was happening to Harper, the rest of the party continued their quick pace toward the main path.

When they arrived on the main path, Snodgrass noticed Harper was missing.

"Where's Harper?"

"He was right behind me," Rizzo said. "Let me go check on him."

When Rizzo went back to get Harper, he immediately plowed into the same sign and landed a couple of feet away from the unconscious detective. Meanwhile, Snodgrass and Lars continued to wait for Rizzo and Harper but they did not appear. As they were waiting, they could see in the distance that Dr. and fake Mr. Delworth were walking toward them. Lars and Snodgrass slowly walked back into the hiking trail behind some bushes so as not to be seen.

"I better go find Rizzo and Harper," Snodgrass told Lars.

Snodgrass ran back into the forest via the hiking trail only to hit his head on the sign like Rizzo and Harper, sending him into a crumpled heap beside his two colleagues. Soon Lars became concerned for his friends and ran onto the hiking trail to find them. He knew where the sign was and soon stumbled onto the pile of human carnage that was near the sign. He tripped over the unconscious Harper and then hit his head on the post.

The next morning, the quartet awoke with lumps on their heads and no further into their investigation than they had been the night before. The four men stumbled back to the park parking lot and got into Harper's car and headed back to their office.

CHAPTER 5
A Double Fake

When they got back to the office there was a message on the boy's answering machine. Despite having cell phones they still maintained a separate phone at the office for which they had an old-fashioned answering machine.

"Hello, this is Mayor Johnson, please meet me tomorrow at 10 am. I would like to discuss some things with you."

"Hmmm...I wonder what the Mayor of Whisby wants to discuss with us?"

"I don't know but we have to get over there in 10 minutes. This message was left last night."

The boys quickly hustled over to the mayor's office which was just across the street. When they entered his office they were a little surprised to see who the receptionist was. It was Svetlana Melanoma from the dentist's office.

"Uh, Ms. Melanoma, what are you doing here?"

"Oh I work for the mayor now." Ms. Melanoma was spying on the mayor of Whisby, trying to find out any secrets she could to send back to Russia.

"You boys can go straight in."

If it were possible, the men could practically rotate their heads 360 degrees to keep ogling Ms. Melanoma as they passed by her.

"Gentlemen, thank you for coming over here on such short notice."

"Yes, mayor, that was no problem. How can we help you?" inquired Snodgrass.

The mayor pulled a folder out of the drawer in his desk and then pulled out a photograph from it.

"This man. I believe he is a Russian spy."

The photograph the mayor was holding up had the image of what the boys believed to be the fake Mr. Delworth.

"This is Vladimir Popoff."

"How do you know that Mr. Mayor?"

"It's a hunch I've been having about him."

"Did you get this information from the FBI?"

"Are you kidding? The FBI is useless."

"What makes you think he's a spy?"

"Well just look at him. Look at those shifty eyes. Look at that overcoat. Typical Soviet-era spy."

"But why do you want us to help?"

"Well, like I said, the FBI is useless."

"You contacted them?"

"Yes, but they won't listen to me."

"Well, what evidence do you have that he's a spy?"

"Well, Ms. Melanoma tells me that he's been hanging around the city hall a lot. She said that one day he came into the reception asking to speak with me. When Ms. Melanoma told him I was at lunch, she got the impression he was trying to lure her out of the office."

"How was he trying to do that?"

"He'd keep making up different emergencies that would get her to run out of the building. One day there was a gas leak, another day there was a fire. Another day there was a Spring Sale at the local department store."

"None of these ruses worked?"

"The Spring Sale almost worked. Ms. Melanoma said she saw an adorable handbag that was fifty percent off."

"Wow, that is a bargain!" Harper exclaimed.

"Plus he's been trying that with other receptionists as well. He recently did this with the receptionist for the city engineer, the receptionist for Councilman Marblehead, Councilman Stalin, and Councilman Lenin."

"You have councilmen who go by the name of 'Stalin,' and 'Lenin'?"

"Why is, that unusual?"

"Well, you made references to the Soviet-era..." Snodgrass paused to see if that would get a rise out of the mayor.

"I don't get your point."

"What would you like us to do Mr. Mayor?"

"I want you to follow this guy and see what he's up to. He's been alarming the staff and I won't tolerate it/"

"Isn't this more of a job for the Whisby police?"

"I told Commissioner McCracken, but he's just ignored me. Says he's planted some men around the city buildings to observe but that's not true. I need you boys to follow this guy and uncover the plot he's making against this great land of ours."

With that Harper stood at attention and began to salute. Snodgrass didn't know whether to copy his actions or slap him over the head.

"Your mayorship, we will proudly follow and uncover any malevolent behavior on the part of this potential spy," Harper said in a military-type delivery.

"Thank you, boys. You make me proud."

Snodgrass wasn't sure what they were committing to but since they were following the man anyway it didn't really matter.

Later that afternoon, after spotting the fake Mr. Delworth boarding the rapid transit at the Whisby station, Harper and Snodgrass jumped aboard just in time to follow him. The train went to various stops and the boys carefully watched the fake Mr. Delworth from one of the backrows of the dining car.

"Will you be dining with us tonight sir?" one of the waiters asked Snodgrass.

"Ah, is there a dinner service on these?"

"Yes, recently implemented by the company headquarters to 'spritz' things up."

"Ah, okay. What's the special?"

"Well, it's a trout almondine with asparagus and baked potato."

"That'll be great. We'll have two of those."

Harper and Snodgrass continued to monitor the movements of the fake Mr. Delworth who was being panhandled in the first row by what looked like a drunk and stumbling Toulouse Lautrec. He was reading a newspaper and was trying to ignore the repeated requests from the bungling con artist.

As the boys were served their meals, and they passed through a tunnel, they lost sight of the fake Mr. Delworth. When the light of the sun illuminated the cabin after passing through the tunnel, the fake Mr. Delworth had disappeared.

"Harper, he's gone. Let's go."

"But I was just starting in on my trout."

"Never mind that, we need to go."

The boys ran through the car looking for the fake Mr. Delworth up and down. When they arrived at the Dillwood station they got off and started looking everywhere they could.

"He couldn't have just vanished into thin air?"

"Maybe he had gone to a different car on the train?" Harper suggested.

"Quick, get back on the train!"

Before the boys could return to the train, it began to pull out of the station.

"Shoot, we missed it!" cried Snodgrass.

"Yes, and that was my first-time eating trout."

"Will you forget about the trout!"

"Okay, I will try."

At that point, Harper had a painful expression on his face like he was trying to put the thought of eating trout out of his mind.

"Will you stop with that!" Snodgrass said, slapping Harper on the chest and then beginning to look around for any trace of the fake Mr. Delworth. Just then he noticed someone resembling their target running through a nearby parking lot.

"Harper, you see that guy over there. Run around to the left, and I will run around to the right, and we'll corner him."

"Got it!"

With that, the two men split their separate ways and ran around the opposite sides of the parking lot. When they met in the middle they ran into the fake Mr. Delworth as planned and collided with him sending him into a nearby Porche.

"Oh no, that poor thing!"

"Oh, he's okay Harper."

"No, I meant the Porche. He's completely broken the sideview mirror."

The boys escorted the fake Mr. Delworth back into the train station and over to a nearby table.

"Okay, Mr. Delworth. Where were you headed?"

"Ah, well, I wanted to go for a sightseeing excursion near Dillwood."

"Likely story," Snodgrass said sarcastically.

"No Snodgrass, I hear the lilies are in bloom in Dillwood. Must be a splendid sight," Harper said with a blissful look in his eyes.

"Okay, enough. We've been trailing you for weeks now and we want to know what your game is?"

"My game gentlemen? Well, my game is this…"

The fake Mr. Delworth began to pull at his face. The boys looked on in horror trying to figure out what he was doing. He continued to tug on his face and as he did so it became apparent that he was wearing some sort of mask.

"What on earth!" Snodgrass cried.

The fake Mr. Delworth, or whoever he was, finally was able to pull the mask off.

"Gentlemen, My name is Sydney Einsteinbagel. I work for the State Department. I've been trailing the same man you have been for the same amount of time."

"So you are a fake…fake Mr. Delworth?" Harper said with a puzzled look.

"You see, we think your employer Dr. Delworth is a Russian spy."

"Wow. Why would she employ us to follow a fake spy posing as her husband?"

"We're not sure but we think it has to do with Solomon Handlemeyer. Solomon Handlemeyer is a KGB operative working for the North Korean government on loan from Albania."

"Wow, sounds more complicated than a European football transfer agreement," Harper said. Snodgrass looked at him with a look of dismay.

"Exactly. Now you boys keep doing what you are doing. We don't want Dr. Delworth and the fake Mr. Delworth to become suspicious."

The agent began to peer around making sure that no one was watching them.

"I will contact you boys with updates, but in the meantime just follow whatever instructions you have been given by your employer."

"Roger that."

As quickly as the fake, fake Mr. Delworth appeared, equally abrupt was his departure, seeming to vanish into thin air.

"Well, I got to get going. I've got play practice tonight." Harper got up and began to leave.

"I thought you finished that Shakespear thing?"

"We decided to shelve that project. We're now doing Death of a Salesman."

"And the fake Mr. Delworth?"

"He's Biff Loman."

"Oh," a perplexed Snodgrass said. "Shouldn't I come with you then if he's in the play?"

"Yeah, I guess so."

The two men began to wonder why they had been following the fake-fake Mr. Delworth all afternoon when had Harper just mentioned that he was in the new play they could have waited to confront him then.

"Harper, I really think you need to get your head examined."

"I think you're right Snodgrass," Harper said with assurance. Of course, Snodgrass was anything be assured.

Meanwhile, at the Delworth estate. Dr. Delworth walks toward a closet in the basement of her house. As she opens the door, in front of her is a man tied to a chair, bound and gagged.

"I'm so sorry Mr. Handlemeyer. I know you are a little uncomfortable right now but I couldn't afford you compromising my little venture." Dr. Delworth smiled as the agent struggled against his bonds.

"Shortly, everything will be taken care of." She smiled again and closed the closet door. She then proceeded back to the living room where she poured herself a brandy.

At a local Mexican restaurant, the boys finished an enchilada dinner special along with a non-alcoholic margarita.

"Let's get going Harper."

"Boy, do you think that margarita was non-alcoholic? I feel a little tipsy."

"You're always a little tipsy. Now let's get going."

Snodgrass paid the check and the boys headed across the street to the Whisby Playhouse and Dinner Theatre.

When the boys arrived the director of the play called all the actors to the stage.

"Hi everyone, I am sorry to say that we were unable to get the rights to Death of a Salesman so we will be doing an adaptation of the play called Death of a Salesperson."

"I find that much more inclusive," a young female stagehand said with a defiant voice.

"Yes, well, we'll see how it goes."

"Ah, Sam, I don't see the actor who is playing Biff Loman…"

"Sorry Harry, the character in this play is called Buff Lomax."

"Okay, well, I don't see the actor who is playing 'Buff Lomax' here."

"That's because he's out sick."

"I'll run his lines for tonight. So let's get started, everyone. Places!"

At that point, everyone took their places either on stage or off. Harper was handed a script for the updated play. He was to play the part of Happy Loman or as it was in the new rendition 'Slappy Lomax.' Harper began to recite his lines…

"I hope Father is meeting his new sales target. You know how things are in the sales world. Every month there's a new quota, a new target."

"Yes, and the widgets are not selling like they used to here in the Northeast."

"Yes, with the cold winter and snow, the trucks and aero craft have been delaying shipments…ah Sam, can I just say 'airplane' or 'aircraft' versus aero craft? Doesn't seem to work."

"Yes, Henri that's fine."

"Thank you, Sam."

As Snodgrass observed what was happening on stage, he noticed a shadow lurking in the rafters above the stage. The mysterious entity seemed to be the same build and make the same movements as the fake Mr. Delworth. Snodgrass slowly descended the aisle toward the stage and slipped behind a nearby curtain.

"But how can a father be blamed for widget sales if the company cannot get them to market?"

"It's a good question Buff. It reminds me of that football game you played in high school against Central High. You were down 7-0 in the fourth quarter. Your tight end had an injury...Sam does that sound right? 'Your tight end had an injury'?"

Snodgrass continued walking around toward the back of the stage and kept his eye on the man who was on the catwalk above.

"What do you mean Henri?"

"Isn't that kind of rude saying that his tight end had an injury?"

"He's referring to the position on the team not the part of the body."

Snodgrass began to look around and found a ladder that was against the back wall of the theatre. He began to climb up to the catwalk.

"It still sounds a little odd. Give me another name of a player's position."

"Okay, halfback..."

"No."

"Fullback..."

When Snodgrass reached the top of the catwalk, he saw the man reaching up and untying a weight used to help raise and lower the main stage curtain. As Snodgrass neared the man he could see his intended victim was Harper.

"No"

"Guard..."

"Hey you, stop!!!" Snodgrass grabbed the man's arm to stop him pulling down on the weight, as he did so both men broke through the wooden railing of the catwalk and plummeted toward the stage.

"Tackle..."

"Ooooh, that one sounds like a football sounding ..."

BOOOM!!!

Everyone turned around to see two men sprawled on top of the couch that was a part of the set furniture. It had been shattered into pieces and both men lay groaning on the remnants of the couch.

"Someone call for an ambulance! These men are in urgent need of medical attention!" The director cried. The stage manager immediately called 9-1-1.

"Snodgrass, what happened? Are you okay?!!!" a flustered Harper asked.

Snodgrass continued to groan and tried to move but he was severely shaken despite having landed directly on one of the couch cushions.

"Snodgrass are you okay?!!!"

"I'm fine Professor Plum...just a little swoozy."

Harper and the stage manager helped Snodgrass over to a nearby chair. He was clearly dizzy and disoriented from the fall. Harper then ran over to the other man. He was smashed all the way to the bottom of the couch having been landed upon by Snodgrass during the fall. It was like he was encased inside the couch that resembled something that an exploded bomb had been inside. Harper and the stage manager tried to pull him up and finally managed to get him clear of the couch.

"Hey, it's Billy!" Harper cried. 'Billy' being the name that the fake Mr. Delworth had used as an actor.

The fake actor having a fake name for his fake personae. The fake Mr. Delworth was in bad shape and the ambulance arrived just in time to take him to the hospital.

While the EMT crew prepared for 'Billy" on a stretcher, Snodgrass was coming around.

"Good thing you landed on Billy Snodgrass!"

"Which hospital are you taking him to?" Snodgrass asked.

"Whisby Memorial," one of the medics said. They then whisked him out of the theatre and into the ambulance and like a shot they were blazing down the street with siren in full force.

"Harper, we better get down to the hospital in case he comes to. We'll need to see what's going on with our Mr. Billy."

Harper agreed. "I'll get the car."

The two men sped down the street and were immediately pulled over by a policeman.

"Where are you boys going in such a hurry the officer asked."

"Good evening officer. We are Harper and Snodgrass, perhaps you've heard of us?"

The officer searched his mind but came up with nothing.

"Anyway, we are from the Harper and Snodgrass Detective Agency and we are currently working on a high-profile case for the government."

"Really, the U.S. Federal government?"

"Ah, well, no. The Whisby Mayor's office.'

"I see. And this business of yours led you to speed?"

"Yes, officer. We are tracking a potential spy who was hurt at the theatre tonight, He was just whisked away to the hospital. Hmmm."

"What is it?"

"Funny expression isn't it? Whisked away. You know like a whisk you use to whisk pancake batter. I wonder how that became a word?"

"Stay on topic, Harper. Officer, we are really in a hurry and need to leave."

"Not until you have explained yourselves."

"Yes, well, like I was saying, we are in pursuit of a possible spy. He is the fake husband of a woman who contracted us to follow him."

"Fake husband?"

"Yes, the woman created him out of her imagination."

"So he's not real?"

"No he's real, or at least, we pretend him to be. You see, the woman was trying to convince her mother that she was married and so in order to do so she produced a fake husband, but then after the mother questioned it she had to produce a real…well, fake one. So she produced a "fake" Mr. Delworth, who also happens to be an actor at the theatre."

"So the pretend husband also pretends to be other people?"

"Yes, precisely."

"But he's also a spy? Maybe he's pretending to be a spy?"

"Well, that's what we're trying to find out," interjected Snodgrass hoping to get the questioning concluded.

"We're acting on the orders of the Mayor of Whisby so we need to get going, officer."

The officer begrudgingly let the pair go and they headed off to the hospital. When they arrived they were surprised to find that there was no fake Mr. Delworth registered there.

"No, sir, we do not have anyone registered by the name of Billy Friendwich."

"Are you sure nurse? The ambulance would have arrived here ten minutes ago."

"No sir, we haven't had any emergency arrivals since about 4 pm…about five hours ago."

Across town, an Emergency Vehicle pulls into the driveway of Dr. Delworth. The attendants pull out a stretcher with the fake Mr. Delworth on it and immediately take him into the house through the garage.

Perplexed, Harper and Snodgrass shake their heads in unison.

"Hey while we here Don, why don't you get yourself checked out? You took a pretty good tumble there."

"Ah, no. I think I'm fine. We need to head over to Dr. Delworth's house and find out what's going on."

The partners left the ER and headed over to Dr. Delworth's house. When they arrived at the doctor's plush mansion; there were no lights on. It looked very eerie. Too still. Too quiet. What was waiting for them inside, they both wondered. They slowly walked up the walkway and peered through the front door window. Nothing. No lights. No movement. Snodgrass turned the doorknob and it was unlocked. He pushed the door open. They both turned on the flashlight on their cellphones and slowly began to walk around the house. They checked the living room, dining room, and kitchen. Apart from the air conditioning unit turning on, there was silence.

After the men had checked out the upstairs bedrooms, they headed downstairs to the basement. Like everywhere else in the house it was pitch black except for their cellphone flashlights. They began to check all around and finally came to a closet. They opened the door and found both Handlemeyer and the fake Mr. Delworth bound and gagged. But before either Harper or Snodgrass could react, they both felt a sharp sting in their necks before falling unconscious to the floor.

CHAPTER 6
New Locations

When Harper and Snodgrass came to, they woke up in some kind of crate. Apart from several drop cloths that they had been bundled up in, there was nothing else inside. They could feel themselves moving along as if they were in a truck bouncing up and down over a road. When the truck finally stopped, they could feel the sensation of being lifted up. They then heard the sound of the crate being moved along by something mechanical like a track. They then heard a door outside of the crate slam shut and the sound as if that door was being sealed.

Everything was silent for the next half hour. Harper and Snodgrass whispered to each other trying to figure out where they were. Suddenly there was a rumbling sound coming from beneath them. It grew louder and louder until the sound was deafening. The crate began to shake violently. It felt like they were inside a rocket of some kind. Then there was an even louder explosion and then the sensation of being lifted very quickly into the sky. The crate was shaking violently and the boys were bouncing from side to side of the crate. After a few minutes, it began to slowly dissipate until they felt a weightlessness. They were bobbing up and down inside the crate.

For the next half hour, the boys floated around the crate. They were enjoying the sensation. But where were they? Some kind of test chamber for space travel? They soon heard sounds like various mechanisms that seemed to be moving the crate. They heard the sound of a door opening or what they thought was a door and again the crate began to move like it was on some sort of track. The crate came to a stop and then they could hear the door close again. For the first time, they noticed in the crate that there was an oxygen tank on one end and it had an open nozzle that was dispensing its contents into the crate. Why would they need oxygen they asked each other.

When the crate came to a stop, they could hear someone or something trying to pry open one end of the box. Suddenly a bright light appeared and the crate was open on one end.

"Come out boys," a female voice said.

The boys were in a stupor and slowly got up and struggled to get their balance. They were very disoriented.

"Welcome to the International Space Station!" It was Dr. Delworth. She was hovering over the open end of the crate in a space jumpsuit.

"Dr. Delworth, what in the world is happening?"

"Not to worry boys. Please come inside and have a look around."

Harper and Snodgrass floated out of the crate by pushing their arms forward and back like they were doing a breaststroke in a pool. They joined Dr. Delworth in the main cabin. There with her were two cosmonauts. One was looking through a telescope and the other seemed to be conducting experiments with a small beaker and test tube.

"Dr. Delworth, why are we here?" a puzzled Don Snodgrass asked.

"Boys, my name isn't Celia Delworth."

"I thought it was Gloria?" Harper questioned.

My name is Tanya Hardingski. I am an operative for Mr. Putin."

"You are a Russian spy!" Harper bellowed.

"Not exactly. I am on a diplomatic mission to secure more funding for the Russian space program. I am specifically working with American and other Western billionaires to fly into space. They pay us a fee and in return, they get the trip of a lifetime."

"But why all this secrecy, why did you put us on a wild goose chase and who were those men we found tied up in your closet."

"Those were actually spies. They are seeking to overthrow the Russian government."

"I thought one of them was working for North Korea or Albania?"

"No, that was just a front. They are British intelligence."

"So why the elaborate story about creating a fake Mr. Delworth?"

"Like I said, he is British intelligence. I wanted you two to follow him to see what he was up to and you did an excellent job."

"But why are we up here?"

"Boys, I want you to come and work for me. I need you to help keep our funding program going. I need men like you to help me and we...I will pay you well."

"Couldn't you have just emailed us that rather than bringing us all the way up here?"

"Currently we are the only ones up here in the space station. It is the most secure place on Earth...well above Earth. No one can hear our conversation."

"Well, we really already have jobs Ms. Hardingski, we have our business, our detective agency."

"Yes, and I want you to continue doing that. I just want you to periodically check out individuals who we think might be a threat to our operation. Again, you will be well paid."

"Does the U.S. government know about this?"

"Of course. When we get those billionaires to pay us millions of dollars, the U.S. government gets a share."

"But what about those men in your closet; what's going to happen to them?"

"Don't worry boys. They won't be harmed. They will be sent back to the U.K."

Harper looked at Snodgrass who was pondering everything that had happened. He nodded to Harper and then spoke.

"Okay, you have yourself a deal."

Snodgrass shook Hardingski's hand and a deal was born. Hardingski then invited the two to a Russian dinner complete with caviar and vodka. The boys later passed out from the vodka and floated around the cabin for hours in an unconscious state, occasionally banging their heads into various parts of the cabin.

The next morning a Russian spacecraft arrived to take Snodgrass and Harper back to Earth. They later arrived at Vladivostok and were greeted by the most beautiful women they had ever seen. The women had donned Russian dresses that looked similar to the outfits on the nesting dolls. They had baskets with what appeared to be Baklava and other assorted pastries. The ladies then led the men to a limousine and the boys were then shuttled over to a nearby airport. They boarded a private jet and flew to Tirana, Albania where they overnighted. They explored the old city and were duly impressed with the Albanian culture.

The following morning, Harper and Snodgrass went down to the café in the hotel to have breakfast.

"Good morning gentlemen, what can I get you for breakfast?" A beautiful blonde waitress asked.

"Boy, your English is immaculate," Harper complimented.

"Thank you. I studied in England for two years."

"You should be working as a translator or some other diplomatic service."

"Yes, I plan to. I just returned from London, so I took the first thing I could find."

"Are you getting off work soon?" Harper asked.

"Yes, I am just doing the breakfast shift and then I am off."

"Could you show us around Tirana? We'll pay you as a tour guide."

"Oh, you don't have to do that. I would be honored to show you around."

"Hey, can you show us the castle of Count Dracula?" Harper asked.

"Harper, you're thinking of Transylvania and not Albania."

"I'm not stupid Don, I was just joking. How about the chocolate factory?"

"That's Hershey Pennsylvania."

"Just testing you Snodgrass!"

"Well, I'm just happy you didn't think we were in Alabama…or Australia."

The trio began to laugh hysterically. Harper decided he wasn't going to ask the waitress to go and look for some kangaroos.

Later that morning, Harper and Snodgrass met Luljeta in front of her apartment. After a tour of the Mercado Pazarl and the Millennium Gardens, they went to Tirana Castle which was originally a castle but had now been transformed into a tourist village with shops and restaurants. It was a pleasant day and they stopped for an expresso at a quaint café near the village center. They sat outside at a table and enjoyed the fresh breeze that was rustling through the village.

"Luljet, Tirana is a lovely city," Snodgrass said.

"Yes, I think you have a wonderful culture here in Albania," Harper added.

Luljet smiled and nodded her head. A waiter arrived with their expressos and Luljet spoke to him in Albanian. She then motioned to the boys to drink up.

"Were you born here Luljet?"

"Yes, about twenty minutes North of the city."

As Luljet spoke, a napkin was blown off the table. Harper reached down to grab it and suddenly a shot rang out, just missing him. Luckily for Harper, had he not reached for the napkin he would have been struck in the head by the projectile. Everyone inside and around the café began to hide behind the tables and chairs. Harper immediately grabbed Luljet and began to lay on top of her. Policemen began to run into the square where the café was and began to hunt for the sniper.

"Haper are you okay?" Snodgrass asked.

"Yes, fine. Just a little shaken up. If that breeze hadn't blown the napkin over I would be dead." Both men turned to see the hole that had been made by the bullet. The bullet had struck the side of the café and pieces of plaster had been broken off by its impact.

"Luljet are you okay?" Asked Harper.

She silently nodded her head. She had an expression of fear on her face. Clearly, this was not an everyday occurrence in Tirana. Harper looked around to see if it was clear and slowly pulled himself off of Luljet. Luljet smiled, she was not offended by the gallantry of Harper.

"Harper, you can get off of Luljet now."

"I just want to make sure the coast is clear. That maniac could still be around."

It seemed an inordinate amount of time before Harper was fully separated from Luljet.

A detective from the Tirana police arrived in a car that looked like it had been made in a 1970s Communist factory. It was very plain and did not fit the current style of Tirana.

"Hello, I am Inspector Akova. Are you boys okay?" the detective asked with a slight accent.

"Yes, yes. Just missed us but we're okay."

Luljet looked like she was still shaken and had her head down.

"Any idea who could have done this?"

"No idea. We are just here for a few hours and will be leaving Tirana later this afternoon."

"Are you part of the U.S. military or government?"

"No, we just own a small detective agency back in the States." Snodgrass did not want to divulge their newly formed partnership with the Russian government.

The boys decided to take Luljet back to her apartment. It was getting late anyway and they would need to head to the airport soon. On the way there, they noticed a man in a black hat and trench coat starting to follow them.

"Harper, I think someone's following us."

Harper at that point then made a wide array of exaggerated movements that would lead anyone to believe he was scouring all areas in a 360-degree rotation.

"I guess I never taught you to be nonchalant when detecting potential interlopers and spies."

The boys told Luljet to pick up the pace as they turned a corner around a building. Snodgrass instructed Luljet not to be alarmed but to start running to the next building. She did as instructed and the trio ran down an alleyway at the side of the building. Behind the building was a large parking lot that led into a park. The trio quickly made their way to the park entrance. As they ran through the park they noticed a large gathering of people off in the distance. When they neared the location they could see a large valley. The people were gathered around the entrance to a zip line. Snodgrass pointed to the zip line entrance and waved for Harper and Luljet to follow him.

When they arrived at the zip line, Snodgrass instructed the man in charge to set them up in a harness. The man asked for money in Albanian.

"How many leks do we give him Luljet? I think it's like a million leks to a dollar right?" Harper said nervously, trying to determine U.S-Albanian currency conversion while keeping an eye out on the person following them.

Luljet smiled a gentle smile and pulled the appropriate amount of leks from his hand and gave it to the man. She also instructed the man that they were in a hurry and needed to go one right after the other. Being in

Albania they did not have strict zip line laws and so the man agreed.

The three were soon barreling down the zip line and began to scream at the top of their lungs, or at least Harper did. While both Snodgrass and Harper were frightened and somewhat disoriented, Luljet was enjoying the zip line as she got to see parts of Tirana she had never seen before. While her nervous companions hoped the ride would end soon, she enjoyed gliding over beautiful gardens, a river where there were little cottages tucked along its banks, and an actual bank and other government buildings, and of course the great and majestic trees they were skirting in and out of.

When they finally reached the bottom they all landed in a net. When they finally freed themselves from the net and popped over its side, the man in the black trench coat and hat was waiting for them.

"Hi, Mr. Snodgrass, Mr. Harper?"

"Yes," said a slightly stunned Snodgrass.

"My name is Ismail Gjondedaj. I'm with the Albanian Foreign Affairs Office. I came to help escort you over to the airport," the man said in impeccable English.

The trio were relieved to find their pursuer was not the gunman who had earlier taken a shot at them. Still somewhat shaken, Snodgrass smiled a force smile and nodded his head.

"Oh, uh, thank you. Can you help us take Luljet back to her apartment first? Also, like to get a little cleaned up after that zip line ride."

"Certainly, my car is over here."

"Why didn't you call out to us when you saw us in town?"

"My apologies but we do not yell here in Albania. It's very impolite."

Snodgrass nodded a forced nod.

Back at Luljet's apartment, she served the boys tea. They made polite conversation but Luljet was not much in the mood for talking. She was still traumatized by the event earlier in the café. Snodgrass excused himself to use the restroom. When he left, Luljet moved closer to Harper and put her hand on his.

"You are a brave man Mr. Harper."

"Please call me Henri. That's On-ree like the French name."

"Oh, that is a wonderful name. I think you are wonderful."

She then reached over to put a peck on his cheek. Harper smiled and then reached over to kiss her on the lips. Before he could do so she grabbed him and pulled him toward her. She embraced him and they passionately kissed. Snodgrass returned from the restroom and the two quickly disengaged from their amorous activities.

"Nice bathroom you have in there. The window over the toilet has a nice view of the city."

"Yes, yes, we think so," Luljet said somewhat flustered. She gave Harper a pouty look of frustration that they couldn't continue. Harper sighed as well. He had no idea if he would ever see her again.

"You said 'We think so.' Someone else lives her?"

"Yes, my mother. My father died some time ago so it is just me and my mother."

"Oh, that's nice. But she's not here now?"

"No, she went to the market. She won't be back until later."

"Ah, okay. Well, Harper we better get going to the airport."

Harper smiled at Luljet and asked if he could contact her in the future. She wrote down her phone number and email address. Harper gave her a wistful look and hugged her. Snodgrass could see something was happening between them.

"Thank you again Luljet, you've been a wonderful host."

Agent Gjondedaj then drove the boys over to the airport.

"I don't want to alarm you boys but we have a good idea of whom took a shot at you earlier today."

"Really who?"

"He's with the FSB."

"FSB?"

"The FSB is the old KGB."

"Wow, he works as a disc jockey?"

"No Harper, it's not a radio station. The KGB was the old security service for the Soviet Union. When communism fell in the early 90s the name was changed to the FSB."

"Okay, so he left one radio station to go to another one."

"No, you moron, I said the Russian security service, and anyway, radio stations use four digits for their call signs."

"Got it, so he works as a disc jockey for a Russian security service."

"No, you don't get it…"

Just then Snodgrass noticed someone walking down the street. It looked exactly like Lars Olafsson the trail creator for the Whisby Parks and Recreation Department.

"Hey Harper, doesn't that man look like Lars?"

"I don't see him, where are you looking?"

"Over there by that shop."

"Oh yeah. What would Lars be doing in Albania?"

"Not sure. Ismail, can you pull over?"

"Certainly," Ismail replied.

Agent Gjondedaj looked for an open parking place by the curb and immediately pulled into the first one he could find. The boys popped out of the car and ran down the street back toward the shop. When they arrived no one was outside. They looked down a nearby alley but no one was there.

"I swear that was Lars," Snodgrass yelled in frustration.

The boys then got back into the car with Agent Gjondedaj and headed for the airport.

The flight back home was relatively uneventful. They arrived in JFK on time got to catch our connecting flight to Whisby."

The boys ran through the terminal trying to find their gate to Whisby.

"I noticed our tickets say JFK to WSY."

"Yeah, those are the airport codes?"

"Ah, interesting. I wonder what airports KGB and FSB are?"

Snodgrass rolled his eyes. There were many times that Snodgrass would roll his eyes after something Harper had said. It was a wonder why his eyes just rolled out of his head and onto the floor.

CHAPTER 7
A Break in the "Case"?

After   Snodgrass and Harper had returned to the United States, they secretly met at their local diner in Whisby to discuss what they would do. Should they trust Dr. Delworth? Should they get in touch with the American agent they had met? Should they order the blue plate special?

"Hi boys, what can I get you today?" said the snarky old waitress Connie who had been at the diner for over 30 years.

"That's a good one Connie. You're a pistol!" Harper said.

"Whatever. So's what y'all have?"

"I'll have the cobb salad and coffee," Snodgrass said.

"And I'll have the usual."

"The usual what?"

"Like I said, a pistol."

"I wish I had a pistol," Connie said as she blew a bubble from the glob of gum she had been chewing and then turned and walked away.

"Okay, Harper, we got to think about what we do next. Do we really want to stay on Celia Delworth's payroll? Is she legit?"

"Let's get in touch with that agent we met at the Whisby train station the other day.

They made arrangements to meet with the agent in a nearby park by city hall. Agent Einsteinbagel told Snodgrass and Harper to meet him by the jungle gym.

Once Harper had finished playing on the gym the men got down to business.

"We met with Dr. Delworth, or should I say Agent Hardingski on the International Space Station."

"Where?"

"The International Space Station."

"Wow, that must've been cool,"

Snodgrass was a little taken aback by Eiensteinbagel's rather juvenile response.

"Yes, it was. But during our meeting she wanted us to work for her. Do some background checks on potential investors of the Russian space program. Isn't this some conflict of interest?"

"Well, yes, but there is a lot of good you can do for your country by working for her. In essence, you can help us keep an eye on her."

"Spy you mean?"

"Correct. We believe that Dr. Delworth, Agent Hardingski is working as a legitimate emissary for the Russian government, but we don't know for sure. She is here legally in the country."

"But she kidnapped two British agents."

"Well, they technically were snooping on Dr. Delworth and were caught. Nothing happened to them other than being sent back to England. Now what happened in Albania?"

"Oh, you heard about that?"

The agent nodded his head.

"Harper, tell Eiensteinbagel what happened."

"Well, it was a nice day in Tirana. The birds were peeping in the trees, the worms were chirping and the squirrels were jumping…"

"Okay get to the assassination attempt!" Snodgrass yelled with frustration.

"Well, we were in this café with a lovely Albanian girl we had just met that morning. We were sipping our expressos, mine was a vanilla late with steamed…"

"Never mind what we were drinking!"

"Anyway, a shot rang out and just barely missed me, hitting the wall right behind me. I grabbed the girl and threw her to the ground and put my body on top of hers."

"Ooooh, interesting. Was she cute?"

Snodgrass was starting to doubt the professionalism of the agent.

"Yes, very cute. Her name is Luljet. She was a beautiful girl. Very intelligent. I would like to see her again."

"But you don't suspect her? You don't think she set the two of you up? Possibly working for Dr. Delworth."

"That's certainly a possibility," said Snodgrass, having not considered that before.

While the three men continued to talk, there were people starting to assemble just outside of city hall. A man placed a podium just outside of the front door.

"I wonder what that's about?" asked Snodgrass.

"The mayor is about to give a speech," Einsteinbagel said.

"Oh, and one other thing. A friend of ours…Lars Olafsson."

"What about him?"

"There was someone in Tirana who looked just like him. I swear it was him."

"Lars Olafsson? Okay, I'll check him out."

"Thanks."

The three men then headed over to the city hall where the mayor was about to make a speech.

"Good afternoon everyone. Thank you for joining me here at the City Hall. What a bright and beautiful day it is. What a bright and beautiful day it is to be an American."

There was a light smattering of applause from the crowd, which had grown to almost a thousand people.

"The reason I am speaking to you here today is that the town of Whisby is really going to be on the map and make an impact to the America of the future! As we grow this great town, we have been inviting various corporations to help with providing income for our citizens and other valuable inputs. We recently brought in Tokyo Motors who have built a small assembly plant for the manufacture of car parts which now employs over one hundred of our fine citizens!"

There was some applause from the crowd, with most knowing that many of those employed were from the competing town of Trelsby as well as Japanese citizens.

"Well today, I would like to welcome from the Soviet Union, I mean Russia, Vladimir Konevshenko! Mr. Konevshenko will be building a new plant here in Whisby, Konevshenko Industries. They will be manufacturing parts for the International Space Station. They hoped to employ another one hundred of our fine citizens at the plant. And why don't we hear from Mr. Konevshenko right now!" The mayor pointed to the front door of the City Hall and out walked a very robust, yet plump balding individual. Somewhat a carbon copy of Leonid Khrushchev from the 1960's, Konevshenko reminded one of the Soviet-era Russian.

"Hello comrades...I mean everybody. I am grateful for the opportunity to speak to you today and announce that Konevshenko Industries will be a great...how do you say...boon to the Whisby economy. We will bring not only great jobs but we will bring our great Russian culture to Whisby. A culture that brought you Tchaikovsky, Russian nesting dolls, and the gulag! I'm just joking about the last one. Anyway, we look forward to getting to know you and hope that this will be a great partnership!"

The crowd became a bit more animated and applauded the Russian businessman.

"Thank you Mr. Konevshenko. We look forward to your partnership..."

"Just then Snodgrass noticed someone in one of the upper windows of the City Hall. As he focused on the image he realized it was Dr. Delworth. Why would Dr. Delworth be in the Mayor's office? Clearly, she would have an interest in Mr. Konevshenko but something seemed not too kosher.

As the mayor made his closing remarks to the rousing anthem of the Beatles, *Back in the USSR*, everyone in the crowd began to disperse.

"Hey Harper, there's Lars, let's run after him!"

The two men quickly spotted Lars in the crowd and before Lars could react confronted him.

"Lars!"

"Oh, hey guys, how's it going?"

"Great, but we saw you last week in Tirana, Albania. Why were you in Albania?"

"Me? In Albania? I don't think that was me."

Just then he dropped a plane ticket out of his pocket and Harper quickly picked it up.

"What's this? Why it's an old plane ticket from Whisby airport to Tirana Albania."

"Oh that. Well, yes, yes I went to Albania. I like going to Albania for my vacation."

"You're sure it's not for another reason...like spying for the Communists?!!!"

"No, no not at all. I really enjoy the parks over in Albania. I often use them as my model to build hiking trails."

"Well you know Snodgrass they did have some really nice parks. Remember the one where we did the zip line? That was beautiful."

Snodgrass gave Harper an incredulous look.

"I find it a bit of a coincidence that you were in Tirana at the same time we were. Perhaps you were there spying on us for Dr. Delworth?"

"No never. I am an American!"

"I thought you were Danish?"

"I am a Danish American!"

"As long as he's not a real Danish, eh Snodgrass?"

"A real Danish?"

"You know, like the pastry...never mind."

"Look guys, I would never betray this great country. It's given me my dream job of creating hiking paths, trails, and walking paths, trails...hiking trails...paths. I would never jeopardize that."

As the boys continued to talk, Snodgrass turned around and looked up at the second-floor window of the City Hall. Now, very prevalently, Dr. Delworth was looking down at him. She shook her head as if to say to leave Lars alone. Snodgrass nodded and then motioned to Harper to leave.

"C'mon Harper, let's get going. Good talk Lars. We'll see you later."

The boys headed over to Khan's Restaurant to meet with Rahul Diwali and his wife Indira. Diwali was an Indian businessman who wanted to go into space and visit the International Space Station. He was a millionaire a thousand times over which meant he was a billionaire and could easily afford the trip to space. Dr. Delworth wanted the boys to meet him and convince him to make the trip.

"Good afternoon boys, My name is Rahul and this is my wife Indira."

"Good to meet you, " Harper said extending his hand.

"Nice to meet the two of you," Snodgrass also extended his hand to shake.

"We hear you two are old hands in space?' Indira said.

"Oh yes, we have been to space and back," Harper said.

"We have experienced space firsthand, and I can tell you there is a lot of it…space that is. In fact, there is so much space that there is little left for anything else."

Snodgrass and the Diwalis gave Harper a slight look of awe.

"So, tell us a little bit about yourselves?" Snodgrass asked the Diwalis."

"Well, we come from the Punjab region of India. I made my wealth in IT."

"Oh IT, I really like it." Snodgrass and the Diwalis looked at Harper a little puzzled.

"I like it...I like IT. You know I like it...IT."

"Yes, Harper thank you for that."

"We have data centers all around India, Dubai, and London. We have some of the best software developers in the world. We create some of the best data mining software."

"Oh, is that where they go underground and dig for stuff?" Snodgrass and the Diwalis decided to ignore that question.

"Anyway, we heard that the Russians were offering trips into space and so we thought we'd check it out."

At that point, the waiter delivered the food to their table. The Diwalis had ordered Butter Chicken with Nan bread and Lamb Briani.

"Here, have some nan bread," Indira offered the boys.

"Boy, for none bread that sure looks like actual bread. Well maybe more like a tortilla."

At that point, the Diwalis decided they wouldn't respond to Harper.

"So what do we need to do to sign up?"

"Well, we will speak to our boss. Do you know of her Celia Del Worth?"

"No, I can't say I am familiar with that name."

"Not to worry. We will work with her and then get back to you. I think we have all of your contact information and we will let you know next steps, costs and so forth."

"Excellent."

"Diwali, Your name sounds like the festival Diwali?" Harper said out of the blue.

"You know about Diwali?" Mrs. Diwali asked in amazement.

"Oh yes, I dated a girl from India once. She took me to a party where they celebrated Diwali."

"Diwali is the Indian festival of lights. How did you like it?"

"Well, it was okay when the lights were on, but then she turned them off and I couldn't find my way around. Long story short, I eventually found my way out of the apartment."

The Diwalis were confused by Harper's story but what else was new?

After the quartet had finished their dinner, they departed the restaurant, and Snodgrass and Harper headed back to the agency. There Snodgrass began to do some background checks on the Diwalis. By background checks, Snodgrass called his contact over at the Whisby Police Department to do the looking for him. Molly Malone was a 10-year member of the Whisby police force and had a crush on Snodgrass. She would do just about anything for him.

"Molly, can you do a background check on Rahul Diwali and his wife Indira for me?"

"Sure Snodgrass, but it'll cost you dinner and a movie."

"Sure, Molly. You get me that info and we'll go out this weekend how about that?"

As Snodgrass hung up the phone, a woman entered the office.

"Luljet?" Harper said in astonishment.

"Yes Henri, it is I, Luljet."

"What are you doing here?"

Luljet immediately ran into Harper's arms and gave him a long passionate kiss.

"I missed you so much. I had to see you."

"You just hopped on a plane and came over?" Snodgrass questioned.

"Yes. I have to say that I have never felt this way before about a man. You see in my country, most men are rough and burley, but not like Harper. He's soft and gentle."

"Yes, he's definitely soft."

"Luljet, I feel the same about you. Since we left Australia…"

"Albania."

"…Albania, I haven't been able to think of anything else."

The couple hugged and then walked over to the couch to continue their romance. Snodgrass could see that three was going to be a crowd and decided he would take Molly on the date that he owed her. He needed a break from the case anyway. But what was the case? The fake Mr. Delworth had been found; a British spy who was surveilling a U.S. citizen who was serving as an envoy for the Russian government on behalf of the International Space Station, who was recruiting billionaire donors who wanted rides into space and who was willing to continue to pay Snodgrass and Harper a stipend to help increase said donations. The "case" had become something different altogether. How were they going to be able to attract more business if they hadn't really solved a case as of yet? Snodgrass could only console himself with the hefty checks Dr. Delworth continued to deposit into the agency's account.

"Harper, why don't you invite Luljet to dinner and you can give her a tour of Whisby."

"Great idea Don. But we have to be quick. I have my play tonight."

"Oh, which play are in?" Luljet asked.

"Death of a Mailman."

"I thought you guys were doing Death of Salesman?"

"We were but we ran into some copyright issues."

"Yes, and then I thought you changed the name to Death of a Salesperson or something else?"

"We did, but the script was working so we came up with a completely different idea."

"You switched Salesman to Mailman?"

"Yes, it's about a disgruntled mail worker who is tired of listening to his wife about his bad career choices so he goes postal on everyone."

"Hmmm, sounds a bit dark."

"Yes, but it's done with a lot of love."

Snodgrass, in his usual manner, rolled his eyes, grabbed his jacket, and bid the couple a fine evening.

After a delightful 10-minute tour of downtown Whisby, Harper invited Luljet to dinner at the finest Italian restaurant in Whisby, *La Girtorio*. It was owned by his friend Dominic Rizzo who greeted the couple as they came in.

"Harper, so great to see you again my friend. And who is this lovely lady?"

"Dominic, I'd like you to meet Luljet. Luljet is visiting from Albania."

"Oh, well I hope you enjoy your stay Miss Luljet. Let me take you to your table."

Rizzo took the couple to one of the best tables in the restaurant. It overlooked the downtown of Whisby.

"You will like this view, Harper. May I recommend the special for today? It's a Chicken Parmigiana, with seasonal vegetables. Also, the house red wine is a perfect compliment. Enjoy!"

"Actually Rizzo, that sounds fine. We'll have two of the specials."

"Grazi mi amigo."

Harper did a double take when Rizzo employed two languages. Rizzo smiled and gave him a wink.

"Well, this is lovely," Luljet said after taking a view of the town.

"You have such a lovely town, Henri. I can see why you love living here."

"Speaking of things that look lovely, Luljet, you look amazing. I thought in Bulgaria…"

"Albania."

"Albania, you looked like the most beautiful woman I had ever seen. And now, you here with me…it's like a dream come true."

"Oh Henri, that is such a beautiful sentiment."

Harper moved his hand so that it was on top of Luljet's hand. She coyly smiled at him. He smiled and his heart was filled. He had several earlier relationships in his life but they either fizzled out or resulted in murder attempts by the prospective mate. No charges had been brought. But Harper was scrappy. He would not let unsuccessful relationships and murder attempts dissuade him from finding love. Luljet was the woman of his dreams and he vowed to make this relationship successful or at least survivable.

Across town, Snodgrass was entertaining Molly Malone at the Capri Bistro.

"Thank you Molly for doing the background checks on the Diwalis. It's much appreciated."

"No worries Don, glad I could help you."

Just then Luigi the waiter walks up.

"Ah, signore Donovan, how are you tonight?"

"Very well Luigi and yourself?"

"Very well, and who is this lovely lady?"

"This is Molly Malone, she's a sergeant with the Whisby police department."

"Well, well, I certainly wouldn't mind being frisked by you madam," Luigi said with a rather absurd grin.

"Yes, well, what are your specials tonight Luigi?"

"Yes, we have a Veal Parmigiana…very good, very succulent. This goes well with our house red wine."

"Great, we'll have two of those."

"Very good sir. I'll be right back with a carafe of the house wine."

"So Molly, what do we know about the Diwalis?"

"Well, they look clean. No fraudulent activities that we can find although they are Indian nationals you cannot be 100% sure on what the Indian government is reporting."

"By the way, 'Diwalis,'? Isn't Diwali the Indian festival of light?"

"From what I understand yes."

"Interesting."

"Why is it interesting?"

" Well, their last name is Diwali."

"Yeah, so?"

"Well, it's like being named Donavan Christmas, or Donavan Thanksgiving. It's just different, plus I don't think Indians are typically named that way."

"You're an authority on Indian culture?"

"Not exactly, but I am familiar with the customs over there. I worked a year in India in the Peace Corps after college."

"Well, well, Molly Malone you do continue to surprise me."

"Oh yes Donavan Snodgrass, I am full of surprises." She gave Snodgrass a wink as their carafe of wine arrived.

"So why do you need this information, Donavan?"

"Well, Harper and I are working for this…shall I say organization. They provide opportunities for billionaires to go into space. This organization has seen that we have a good detective agency and thought we would be ideal for vetting potential candidates to go into space."

"Hmmm…but you just started this agency about six months ago."

"Yeah so?"

"And you have already built up that kind of reputation?"

"I guess so. We are very competent like the sign says."

"Yes, but this seems like a pretty high-profile job for such a small agency. I mean why are they not contacting the government or some law enforcement agency to do the checking?"

"I guess they just don't want too many eyes on this. I mean Dr. Delworth is working for the Russians after all."

"Are you sure this is all legit?"

"I'm not sure, but we are trying to find out. In the meantime, we are in touch with an agent from the U.S. government. He wants us to continue observing the process and especially Dr. Delworth."

"Be careful Donavan. Don't want anything to happen to you." As she said this, Molly put her hand on Donavan's and smiled at him. Donavan reciprocated.

Meanwhile, across town, Harper and Luljet continued to have dinner.

"Oh no,"

"What is it?"

"I'm running late to get ready for the play."

"We better get going then."

"Rizzo, the check!" Harper yelled across the restaurant.

After paying, Harper grabbed Luljet by the hand and they raced across the town center over to the Whisby Theatre. He told Luljet to wait for him in the audience as he made his way to the dressing room to get his hair and makeup done.

Thirty minutes later the play began. The curtain rose and a floodlight slowly illuminated the stage. It was a set of an imaginary office at a local post office. Emerging from a doorway was Harper, playing Spiff Loman, the main character.

"It seems the mail will never stop. It keeps coming and coming. I've never seen it like this."

To his right, coming through another doorway was another gentleman playing Spiff's boss.

"Yes, Loman. It's the time of the year. You've been working here twenty years, you should know that."

Luljet was near the front row of the theatre and was impressed by the scene.

"You don't have to tell me, Fred, I am perfectly aware of the seasons and the amount of mail. It just seems we have more than usual. We've got more large boxes this year, more freight, more express mail. It's piling up. But it's also a philosophical metaphor I am conveying. The idea that the mail will never stop. The idea that the world never comes to a stop and rests. It just keeps going and going. When do we all just stop and shut everything down? Take a moment to reflect. Take a moment to smell the flowers."

"Oh, I see."

"It's like a river that never stops. It never dries up. A river of mail that flows through the North Central Region; Cincinnati, Toledo, Youngstown, Pittsburgh, Cleveland, sometimes, I just can't take it!"

As Harper said the line, "I just can't take it!" something immediately fell from above the stage and stuck Harper on the head. He fell over to the angst of the theatre audience. When everyone realized what had happened the lights immediately came up and everyone began to gasp in unison. The curtain came down and the stagehands rushed onto the stage. Luljet was concerned for Harper and tried to run backstage.

When the stagehands arrived at Harper's side they could see it was one of the counterweights from up above the stage that had its rope cut, causing the sandbag to plummet to the stage. Harper was out cold and the stage manager used his cell phone to call for an ambulance.

Luljet ran to Harper's side and began to hold his head up to see if he would come to. Another stagehand brought out some smelling salts to see if that would revive him.

"Stand back everyone," It was the new director 'Sam Bernard' (AKA the fake Mr. Delworth).

Luljet, not knowing who he was immediately moved back from Harper.

"Let me take a look. I also have had some medical training." The fake Mr. Delworth, who we now know was an undercover British spy who had been subdued by Dr. Delworth and sent back to the UK, began feeling for a pulse.

"He has a pulse and is breathing but clearly he has suffered some head trauma. Hopefully, the ambulance will be here shortly."

Within a few minutes, an ambulance pulled up and the two attendants quickly moved Harper inside of it. Luljet was able to accompany Harper to the hospital.

When they arrived at the hospital, they rushed him to the Emergency Room where a doctor was waiting. They did some scans and x-rays and did not find anything of consequence. Snodgrass and Molly Malone, having been contacted by Luljet also arrived at the hospital. Luljet met them in the waiting room.

"Luljet, what happened?"

"Oh, it was terrible Don. Henri was giving this great performance when all of a sudden he was struck by one of the sandbags that was hanging above the stage. I'm waiting for the doctor to let us know what's happening."

Luljet went over and hugged Don, who in turn tried to console her.

"I'm sure he'll be okay Luljet."

As he said that, the ER doctor came out.

"Hi folks, are you the family of Henri Harper?"

"Sort of, I'm his best friend, Donavan Snodgrass."

"Okay, Mr. Snodgrass. We think Henri will be okay. He has suffered a concussion and we'll need to keep him overnight for observation but we think he will be fine. As his best friend we will need you to come get him tomorrow and keep an eye on him and alert us to any abnormalities he might experience. Are you able to contact his family?"

"Henri doesn't have family per se. His parents have passed away. He has an uncle in Spicer but that's about it."

"He's not married or has been married?"

"No."

"Can we see him?"

"And who are you?"

"My name is Luljet. I am a friend of his."

"Why don't you come back in the morning Luljet and you can see him then."

The trio turned and walked out of the ER. Snodgrass told the ladies that he wanted to go over to the theatre and take a look around. He asked Luljet to go back to his apartment which Molly was not too thrilled to hear. Molly volunteered to take Luljet there and help her get situated.

From the Whisby Memorial Hospital, Snodgrass drove over to the Whisby Theatre. He went backstage and found a man sweeping up the stage floor.

"Good evening."

The old man looked up in astonishment, not thinking anyone would be around at that hour.

"Oh, good evening. You startled me a little."

"Sorry about that. My name is Donavan Snodgrass. I'm a private investigator. I heard you had a little excitement here tonight?"

"Oh, yes, there was a production going on here. I think it was Death of a Salesman or Death of a Milkman...I couldn't keep it straight they changed the name so many times. And me, I had to keep changing the marquee outside multiple times."

"I see. And I heard there was some other kind of excitement?"

"Oh yes, there was a lady who thought she had left three tickets in will call. Well, it turns out she only purchased two and so there was a big ruckus about paying for the third one. The third ticket was for their cousin who was coming from out of town...Kansas, Kentucky, one of those places I think..."

"No, I was referring to the accident."

"Oh, yes, There was this delivery truck that was dropping off a couch for the stage. It backed up right into the loading dock and..."

"No, I mean the actor who got hit in the head with a sandbag."

"Oh, that. Yeah, sad thing that. I hope he's okay?"

"Yeah, I just came from the hospital. He has a concussion but should be fine."

"Oh, that's good news."

"Do you mind if I have a look around, Mr...."

"You can call me Paul. Paul Stevens. I'm sort of the handyman around here. Yeah, that's fine. Look around all you need to."

"Thanks, Paul. Do you know where the sandbag is that hit the actor?"

"Well, I remember the director moving it."

"The director?"

"Yeah, Samuel S. Bernard."

"Why did he move it?"

"Not sure. All I know is he moved it."

"Do you know where I can find Mr. Bernard?"

"Well, they announced that given the circumstances they would need to cancel the rest of the shows. He then said he was heading out of town."

"Do you know where that might be?"

"Not a clue."

Snodgrass then ascended a ladder that took him above the stage to a catwalk. He walked several feet to where he thought Harper might have been and discovered a rope that had been severed.

"I think I found the rope that was holding up the sandbag," Snodgrass said, raising his voice so that Paul could hear.

"Looks like it has been cut through with a knife."

"So no accident then?"

"Not likely. Did you see anyone unfamiliar walking around during the play?"

"Not that I can say. I mean there were a lot of people milling about during the production."

Snodgrass headed down the stairs back down to the stage.

"I sure would like to take a look at that sandbag."

"Can't help you there I'm afraid."

"I wonder why the director would have taken it."

Paul shrugged his shoulders and shook his head.

"Okay, well thanks, Paul. I'll be going."

Paul nodded and resumed sweeping the stage.

As Snodgrass passed through the front lobby, he noticed a glass enclosure on the wall. Inside the enclosure were some photographs. As he got closer, he could see that several of the photos were of the main cast including Harper. Another photo though really caught his attention. It was that of the director whom he immediately recognized as the fake Mr. Delworth. He had died his hair a dark black color, but apart from some thick rimmed glasses, it was definitely the fake Mr. Delworth. But why was he back in the U.S.? Was Dr. Delworth lying? She had said he was sent back to the U.K. Things were not adding up.

Snodgrass got back to the apartment a little after 10 pm. He offered Luljet his bed and he opted for the living room couch. Snodgrass ensured there were clean sheets on the bed and showed her the bathroom where she could do her ablutions and shower.

"It's not much but it's a warm soft bed."

"Oh don't worry Don. It's lovely. Good night."

"Good night Luljet. We'll check on Harper first thing in the morning."

A smile and a twinkle in her eye emerged from the thought of seeing her Henri. She seemed to be a girl in love. Snodgrass contemplated whether the time they all had spent in Tirana was enough for someone to fall in love. Not an expert on the subject, Snodgrass chalked it up to infatuation.

Snodgrass made himself some tea, read for a half-hour, and then watched TV. He slowly fell asleep with a late-night detective show. *Shelby and Sons,* what he would profess publicly as not an accurate detective show. Secretly he loved it. A man owning his own detective agency who had his sons help him run it. That would be his dream. To one day hand down his agency to his son or sons. It made him muse about his relationship with Molly Malone. Was she marriage material? Molly was great. She was like a female version of Snodgrass only more intelligent. Maybe he should employ her instead of Harper he thought. *The Snodgrass Family Detective Agency*?

With that thought, she gave Molly a call.

"Hi Molls, how you doing?"

"I'm doing well. How did you get on at the theatre?"

"Pretty good. I did find one thing of interest. The sandbag that hit Harper is missing. The janitor said that the director took it."

"The director took it. Why?"

"Not sure other than he was the man we pursued at the start of this case. Dr. Delworth, the lady I told you about who is a Russian emissary said it was her husband. She had suspected him of having an affair and that she wanted us to follow him. At least that was the initial story. Turns out he's actually a spy for MI-6 in England. She just wanted us to follow him around so she could figure out what he was up to. She then kidnapped him and sent him back to England."

"Wow, this sounds intriguing."

"Yeah, Harper and me went over to her house and found him and some other guy bound and gagged in one of her closets. The next thing we knew, after having been knocked out, we were in space and working with Dr. Delworth on the International Space Station. She wanted us to work for her vetting prospective space travelers who would pay the Russians millions just for the opportunity to go to space."

Molly was starting to wonder if Snodgrass had been hit in the head with a sandbag. Just then, Snodgrass heard something.

"Hey Molls, I'll call you back."

Snodgrass put his cell phone down and started to walk into the kitchen. He then walked near the hallway. He had definitely heard something. Maybe Luljet was stirring and moving around the room. The next thing he heard was a blood-curdling scream. He immediately ran into Luljet's room and was struck on the head with something.

As Snodgrass lay on the floor of the bedroom, he slowly came to. As he came to, he could see Luljet struggling with a man in a mask. He slowly regained his bearings and helped Luljet. Together, they soon subdued the man in the mask.

"Who are you?!!!" Yelled Snodgrass as Luljet turned on the light. The man was clad head-to-toe in black, resembling a ninja. Snodgrass took off his baklava.

"It's the fake Mr. Delworth!" Exclaimed Snodgrass.

"No, I'm Agent Travers from MI-6. I've come to warn you about…"

Before the agent could speak further, Luljet had taken one of her scarves and began to wrap it over his mouth. She took another scarf and bound his hands behind his back. Snodgrass was duly impressed with her efficiency.

"Thanks, Luljet. I don't think this man can be trusted. Let's take him over to Dr. Delworth's house."

Snodgrass and Luljet loaded the agent into the back of their van and headed over to Dr. Delworth's. Dr.

Delworth was at the door waiting for them when they arrived.

"Dr. Delworth, this is Luljet. A friend of ours from Albania."

"Nice to meet you Luljet."

"Nice to meet your Dr. Delworth. A lovely home you have here.

"Why thank you my dear. Well, great work you two. I thought we had gotten rid of our spy here but clearly he doesn't like to stay where he belongs. We'll have to teach him a little lesson. Svetlana!"

Just then a tall, blonde woman appeared. Snodgrass was somewhat shaken by her appearance. He was sure he knew her. Her name came to mind – Melanoma, the assistant at Dr. Greenlaw's dental practice. Could it really be her?

"Svetlana, please take our British guest and secure him downstairs."

"Svetlana," nodded and forcefully ushered the English spy downstairs.

"Don, can I have a word?"

"Ah, certainly."

Snodgrass nodded to Luljet and then followed Dr. Delworth out of the kitchen and up the stairs to her study.

"First off, great work with the agent there and secondly, excellent work with the Diwalis. The Diwalis have agreed to a trip to space and have given us 10 million dollars. You have done a great job. And as a little thank you, with more of this to come…"

Dr. Delworth handed Snodgrass a check. It was for $100,000. His hand started to tremble as he tried to count the number of zeros.

"Are you sure you want to give us this much Dr. Delworth?"

"Oh yes. Without you, we would probably wouldn't have gotten the Diwalis. They were very impressed with you. They said they both really enjoyed Harper's entertaining ways."

"Yes, well Henri does like to entertain."

"How is he by the way?"

"He seems to be in stable condition. We are going to the hospital in the morning."

"Well, give him my regards. By the way, please keep our business away from Luljet. I'd prefer there be just a few people aware of what we are doing. Please don't let any of your other friends know as well. Snodgrass began to think of Rizzo, Lars, and Molly who all had some knowledge of what was happening.

"Ah, yes, of course. I will keep it on the down low as they say."

"On the what?"

"Uh, never mind."

Snodgrass turned for the door to the study but then stopped and turned around.

"You won't be interrogating or hurting the spy will you?"

"Absolutely not. He is just a fly in the ointment. There's someone in MI-6 who thinks this emissary work we are doing is something much more nefarious. We will do with him what we did last time. Svetlana will load him into one of our cargo planes heading to Albania. It will make s short stop in London, where Svetlana will drive him to a field, drop him off and someone will eventually find him after she tips them off. By then Svetlana will be well on her way to Tirana."

"Why Albania?"

"Well, they are a good ally of ours. That's why on your way home from the space station you made a stop there. We have colleagues in Albania that help us with what we are doing."

Snodgrass began to ponder the Albanian connection. There seemed to be a lot of things related to Albania that were associated with the case. Like Luljet. Could Luljet be a spy? No that was impossible. They had just randomly picked the café where she was working. Or did they? He did remember asking the hotel front desk clerk for a recommendation for a local street café. Could he also be working for the organization?

CHAPTER 8
Life of the (Communist) Party

The next morning, Snodgrass and Luljet went to the hospital to visit Harper.

"There he is!" Snodgrass exclaimed as they walked into the room. Harper was up and watching TV.

"Oh hey, guys. How you doing?"

"How are we doing? How are you doing?"

"The doc says I have a concussion, they are just looking at some other tests but think I can go home later today."

"That's fantastic!"

Luljet walked over to Harper and planted a long passionate kiss on his lips. Snodgrass became a little uncomfortable with the exchange but guessed that was how they do things in Albania.

"I really missed you," Luljet said.

"I missed you too. Don, any ideas of what happened last night."

"Oh boy well let me tell you. A lot happened last night. First off you of course got hit in the head. Turns out your director was behind it."

"What Bernard?"

"Bernard was the fake Mr. Delworth. Didn't you suspect something?"

"Oh no," Harper shook his head trying to remember any episodes where Bernard would have betrayed his identity.

"Anyway, last night he tried to break into Luljet's room. And we caught him."

"Hmmm, I wonder why he did that?"

"Oh, he was probably sniffing around for things about the Russian space program. I'm sure that was it." Luljet said.

"Well, we didn't really have time to interrogate him. We took him over to Dr. Delworth's house where she was planning on sending him back to the UK."

"A persistent little bugger huh?" Harper said, concerned that he hadn't recognized the agent.

"And an even greater thing is that Dr. Delworth, thanking us for our work on the case as well as bringing the Diwalis onboard the space program, gave us 100,000 dollars."

"You're kidding!"

"No, we can go get that condo we had our eye on and get out of our apartments."

"Wow, things are really looking up Don."

That afternoon, after Harper was discharged from the hospital, the trio headed over to the Whisby Heights condominiums on the north side of town overlooking the Whisby River. They made a deposit on a condo and then headed into town to buy furniture and other sundries for their new home. Luljet was of course a great help. She decided on the décor and what carpets and furniture to buy.

Harper's contribution to the new condo was a wall map that he purchased. It was a map of the world. He especially liked to look at where Albania was and was amazed about how far away it was from the United States.

They made some final purchases at a local CostClub and then headed to their brand-new condo. It was spacious with two bedrooms and, a large living room, dining room, and kitchen, and a balcony that looked over the Whisby River. It was paradise. Luckily they had been renting apartments from Rizzo, and apart from a $500 early exit fee to their lease, they were able to move out right away.

That night they decided to have a housewarming party. All of their friends were there. Snodgrass had purchased several bottles of champagne and with Harper's music blasting from the new stereo he purchased the party was well under way. Luljet was dancing up a storm and was joined by Harper, who fancied himself as the new up-and-coming Tom Jones. Snodgrass slow danced with Molly, even though the beat required a much more frantic pace. When Rizzo arrived he had several waiters from his restaurant bring in some food.

As Snodgrass had more and more to drink, he decided to invite everyone he knew; The Diwalis, Dr. Delworth, Svetlana Melanoma, Rizzo, Lars, Molly, Dr. Greenlawn and even Agent Einsteinbagel, whom he introduced to everyone as his cousin from Cincinnati.

"Do you have anything by Ravi Shankar?" Mr. Diwali asked Harper. Harper shook his head, content to keep blasting the Police (the band). Speaking of the police, even Captain Thompson from the precinct was invited to the party.

The party was going well and many people mingled and got to know each other.

"Oh, you're from Albania?" Rizzo asked Luljet.

"Yes, it's a beautiful country."

"Yes, my relatives and ancestors are right across the Adriatic in Italy."

"Oh, yes, I love Italy…the culture, the sites, the food. It's fantastic! All we have in Albania is lamb to eat."

"Oh, I know. I remember my cousin said when he went to Greece and Albania, the only thing he would eat was lamb. He loves it though. He's a real glutton for mutton, my cousin."

Snodgrass wandered over to Svetlana to see how she was doing.

"How did everything go in London?" Snodgrass asked Svetlana.

"The baggage was dropped off safely. I understand MI-6 located it fairly quickly."

"Excellent. Another drink my dear?"

Svetlana nodded. She was stunning. She must have been 6' 1" tall. She wore a tight, yellow, form-fitting mini-skirt with matching high heels. While sometimes demure, most people knew not to get on her bad side. She was an expert in Judo. She also had a blackbelt in Karate. She was also brilliant with a degree in engineering from Moscow University. She was the full package and anyone could see why she was under the employ of Dr. Delworth. Or was she under the employment of Dr. Greenlawn? Were Dr. Greenlawn and Dr. Delworth working together? The questions kept flowing into Snodgrass' brain.

Later, someone suggested that they all play Pictionary. Two teams were created, one for Team Snodgrass and one for Team Harper. With a flip of a coin, Team Harper went first.

Luljet handed Harper a card with the word "espionage" on it. Harper thought for a moment and began to draw. He drew a rectangular shape and then inside of that shape put multiple dots.

"A radio!" Dr. Delworth yelled. Harper quickly shook his head.

"A moldy piece of Danish!" Lars exclaimed. Again Harper shook his head.

"A rectangular pizza!" Luljet offered. Harper again shook his head. He then turned to look closely at his work and began to shake his head feeling that it would be difficult to guess what he had drawn.

"Snodgrass, I would like to request that I switch to charades."

"Request granted," Snodgrass replied. The way that Snodgrass and Harper played Pictionary was that if the pictures they drew were not very good, they could instead act out the word on the card. The point is that Snodgrass and Harper were not very good artists. Then why even bring Pictionary into the picture so to speak, you ask yourself? Well, it's just another one of the great mysteries of Snodgrass and Harper. And just stop asking so many questions.

Next, Harper ran over to the curtains that covered new French Windows overlooking the Whisby Falls. Harper was now in his element – acting. He appeared to be hiding behind the curtains and then he would periodically peek out from behind them.

"You are engulfed in satin sheets and you are trying to escape?" Dr. Delworth yelled.

Snodgrass looked at her with contempt. "It's only one word Dr. Delworth"

"Oh yes of course. Sorry."

"You're a Peeping Tom!" Molly practically screamed.

Harper shook his head and then jumped up onto the back of a nice leather couch that Snodgrass had just purchased. The couch was against the wall and Harper then used it to look like he was stalking someone, slowly walking on the top of the couch with his back firmly against the wall.

"Harper, do you really need to use my couch that way?" Snodgrass grimaced.

As he was moving along the wall, Harper lost his balance, grabbed onto the wall-mounted big-screen TV, accidentally ripped it from its mounting, then did a sort of pirouette, and then came crashing down on to the Pictionary easel. Luckily the easel with all of the drawing paper cushioned Harper's fall, as well as prevented any major damage to the TV.

"Oh no, Harper! Is the TV okay?!!!" Snodgrass yelled. The big game with Tech and State is on Saturday!"

Harper seemed to go into a trance as Luljet tended to him.

"Henri, are you okay?" She asked.

Harper smiled but then began to hallucinate. He began to imagine that he and Luljet were on vacation in Italy. They were driving a sportscar through the streets of Capri. Luljet had sunglasses and a scarf in her hair. She couldn't take her eyes off the famous Italian actor Henri Harper. He then imagined taking a bend too quickly. He couldn't turn in time and the sports car went sailing over the side of the cliff.

"No!!!!!!!!!!!!!!!!!" Harper screamed.

"Henri are you okay?" Luljet asked. Harper finally came to. He shook himself off, rising from the crumbled heap of Pictionary easel, paper, TV components, and wire as well as pieces of drywall.

"Yes, whose turn is it?" He said in his disoriented delirium.

Rizzo went next for Team Snodgrass. Luljet handed him a card with the same word that Harper was using close to a half hour earlier with no result. He looked, nodded, and then began to think of how he would get everyone to make the correct guess. He then raised his hand and raised his index finger.

"One word," the crowd said in unison.

After putting the easel back together again, he took the felt pen and began to draw. He wasn't the best artist and so he drew two stick figures. One appeared to be standing while another was close to a line, representing a wall with his ear placed up against it.

"Eavesdropping?" yelled a drunk Snodgrass.

Rizzo nodded his head and motioned for more responses. Almost in unison, everyone at the party yelled the same word, "Espionage." Everyone quietly looked around like a secret had been let out. Was everyone at the party a spy? Clearly, many participated in the quiet art of espionage, but who were they?

The rest of the party went by quickly with many people hoping to avoid eye contact or conversation. Each one began to make their excuse to leave for the evening with Snodgrass and Harper bidding them a fond farewell.

"Well, that was quite an evening," Harper said a little out of breath.

"Yes, very interesting. I think we didn't get any closer to finding out who is really pulling all the strings here."

"Strings?" Harper questioned. It immediately sent him into a vision of various strings that were strewn across various places. They were jumbled and some of them looked like Silly String.

"Yeah, who is really running this operation?"

"Well, we are being paid by Dr. Delworth so she's the one in charge." Harper reasoned.

"I don't believe Dr. Delworth is doing anything nefarious," Luljet quickly interjected.

"Well, she's basically paid for all of this. By the way, when are you getting your place Harper?"

"Not sure. I do like Whisby Heights. Maybe I'll get a place here. Anyway, I think I better head home."

There was an awkward moment where the three of them were looking at each other. Snodgrass bent his neck in Luljet's direction as he looked at Harper with a questioning look.

"Are you okay here Luljet? Otherwise, I can have you over to my place. I'll take the couch."

"I don't want to impose. I could always get a hotel."

"No, no, you come home with me."

Luljet and Harper bid Snodgrass a good evening and they headed over to Harper's place.

Once they arrived at Harper's apartment, he immediately ran in and tried to find some clean sheets. He quickly made up the bed and replaced the pillow covers.

"Ah, here you go Luljet. All nice and clean."

"Um, did you want to join me, Henri?"

"Oh, uh, I would love to but I don't think that would be a good idea."

"Okay, but you are more than welcome," she said with an alluring stare. Harper started to choke up. He desperately tried to clear his throat.

"Thank you. I would love to join you but I think it best I just stay on the couch."

"Such a gentleman," she said. She then walked over to him and planted a long passionate kiss on his lips. When she moved back to get his reaction, she began to giggle. It looked like her kiss had put him into a trance which was more or less the case. What seemed like ten minutes later, Harper let out a sigh. He realized that Luljet had closed the door to his bedroom. He turned and looked at a very sparse and unwelcoming couch. He found a blanket and was soon wrestling with his decision as well as with various pillows on the couch.

CHAPTER 9
A Final Gathering

The next morning, Luljet found Harper making breakfast for her. She came out in Harper's pajamas that were a little big on her but nonetheless gave her a sexy and sultry appearance.

"Wow, you look great," Harper said with his tongue practically dropping to the floor.

"Why thank you, Henri," she said, then giving him a long kiss which he accepted without hesitation.

"Is this a typical American breakfast?"

"Oh yeah, flapjacks, scrambled eggs and bacon."

"Looks great."

While Harper continued making breakfast, Luljet walked back to the bedroom. From his peripheral eyesight, he could catch of glimpse of Luljet standing in the middle of his bedroom. He could see her dropping the pajama shirt and then placing it on the bed. She then made her way over to the shower. He noticed that she seemed to be looking through some of his things as she went into the bathroom. He heard the shower start. He could hear her start to sing. It sounded like some sort of Albanian folk song. It sounded beautiful. He never imagined falling in love with an Albanian girl. Was he really in love? He felt something was happening. If not love then it was very much a strong attraction. But who was she? Did he really know her? Why was she here in Whisby?

"So what's on the agenda for today?" Luljet said, fresh from her shower and drying out her long flowing blonde hair.

"Well, Snodgrass and I have a meeting with the mayor and Mr. Konevshenko."

"Oh, can I come along?"

"I don't see why not,"

After a fabulous American breakfast that Harper had made, the couple headed over to Snodgrass' new condo. They met Snodgrass and Molly and then headed over to City Hall for their meeting.

When they arrived at reception they were told to go to the second floor. They then walked down a long hallway that led to the main conference room. The mayor greeted the quartet before they could enter.

"Ladies, I hope you don't mind but if you could wait out here that would be appreciated," the mayor said. The ladies nodded and then took a seat at a nearby table.

"Sorry ladies. I promise you we will have a nice lunch over at Rizzo's later.'

The girls smiled at each other, nodding in agreement.

The mayor then ushered the boys into the conference room. As they entered, they saw Mr. Konevshenko at one side of the table, and at the far end of the table someone was sitting in a large executive-style chair, but they could not see who it was as his back was turned to them.

"Glad you could make it Messrs. Snodgrass and Harper."

"Messrs.?" Harper thought to himself.

The man began to slowly turn his chair toward them. There in the chair, petting a chihuahua, that was in his lap, was the fake Mr. Delworth.

"Who exactly are you?' Snodgrass asked.

"My name is Walter Wycliffe. I am an operative for MI-6."

"Yes, that's what Dr. Delworth told us. She said that you were an annoyance and that she needed to get you out of the way of her project."

"Yes, that's true, but I am an annoyance to her because I know she is a Russian spy."

"A Russian spy?!!!" exclaimed Harper.

"Yes, and I am here to finally unmask all those who are part of her espionage network."

"Espionage?"

"Yes, her spy network."

"Ah, " Harper finally understood what espionage meant.

Just then, Dr. Delworth marched in.

"I need to see the mayor…oh no, it's you!!!" Dr. Delworth shouted as she saw Walter Wycliffe.

"Dr. Delworth, or should I say, Dr. Wycliffe?"

Everyone looked on in confusion at that title. Just then Luljet ran into the room.

"Luljet, you need to wait outside!" Harper warned her.

"Oh, that's fine, Mr. Harper. Luljet here is a spy as well, working for agent Konevsberg."

"Konevsberg? Who is Konevsberg?" asked a completely stunned Snodgrass.

"That is your dearly beloved patroness Dr. Delworth."

"I thought her spy name was Hardinski?" Snodgrass questioned.

"Yes, that is one of many aliases she uses."

"And Luljet is a spy too?" a dispirited Harper asked.

"Yes, Luljet is her right-hand gal. That's what I was trying to tell you the other night at your apartment Mr. Snodgrass before I was incapacitated by her."

"Yes, I remember. We caught you breaking into my apartment. But you were trying to warn me?"

"Yes, exactly."

"That's a wild story, Mr. Wycliffe. I think your imagination is running overtime."

"Just then, Lars the Trail Maker ran in.

"Don't believe her Snodgrass. It's all true. That's why I was in Albania the same day you were. I was tracking our Ms. Luljet here."

"I thought that was you, Lars."

"So you don't make trails for a living?" asked Harper.

"Yes, I do, but that is more of a hobby. Something I do in my spare time."

"Wow, that's pretty cool."

"Yes, it is."

"Well, this has all been very enlightening gentlemen, but I think that it's time for me to leave," Dr. Delworth aka Agent Konevsberg said as she produced a gun from her coat pocket.

"I wouldn't try that," Lars said as he pulled a gun out that had been lodged in the back of his jeans.

"Put the gun down Lars," said Luljet as she was now pointing a gun at Lars.

"Put that down Luljet," it was Agent Einsteinbagel who had just entered the room.

"My dear friend, I wouldn't do that." Now Mr. Konevshenko pulled out a gun and was pointing it at Agent Eiensteinbagel.

"Boy, this is getting tense," Harper said to Snodgrass.

"I think that's an understatement."

"I wouldn't do that," Agent Wycliffe said.

"Where's your gun?" Konevshenko asked.

"Right here. This is not a real chihuahua but a carefully disguised AK-47."

"Well at least it's a Russian gun," Konevshenko mused.

"Looks like we are at a bit of a standstill," Dr. Delworth said.

"Not anymore doctor."

"It was Svetlana Melanoma."

"Everyone drop your guns," Svetlana demanded.

"You drop your gun," yelled a perturbed Mr. Diwali who entered the room with his wife.

"It's the Diwalis!" Harper cried as if the tide had turned on their side.

At that point, the capacity of the conference room was starting to be exceeded which would gain the wrath of the local fire Marshal if he ever found out.

"We might want to take this outside," the mayor suggested, given the capacity of the room.

"Shut up Johnson. You are my puppet and you will do as I tell you!" Dr. Delworth yelled.

"Don't move Agent Konevsberg," if it were possible to fit any more people in the room it was Harper's dentist, Dr. Greenlaw.

"Excellent work Agent Carmichael," Agent Wycliffe said.

"Who is Carmichael?' asked Harper.

"He is."

"My dentist is Agent Carmichael. Are you really a dentist?'

"No, not really."

"And you took out my tooth?"

"Yes, had to make it look real. Otherwise, Agent Melanoma might suspect."

"Does that mean I need to go back to the dentist?" Harper asked while rubbing his cheek.

"Enough of this, I am leaving," Dr. Delworth said as she opened fire. Everyone hit the floor. Several of the Western agents opened fire as well. The room was tiny, maybe 40 x 40 and there was very little room to have a gunfight. But fight they did. Using the incredibly sturdy executive-style chairs, made by the Richfield Executive Chair Manufactures, located in Richfield, Ohio, the various agents were able to take cover behind them. A spray of bullets was sent all over the conference room. It soon became executive-style chair to executive-style chair combat. The chairs were made of sturdy stuff and could easily deflect gunfire. The battle raged for several minutes while Snodgrass and Harper took refuge behind a portable dessert table that had been rolled in by a waiter.

After ten minutes the battle finally came to an end.

"Harper, what do you see?" Snodgrass asked.

Harper slowly emerged from underneath the dessert table. At first, he could not see anything as there was smoke everywhere. When it finally cleared he saw a terrible sight. Bodies were strewn everywhere. As Snodgrass emerged he too saw the carnage.

"I don't see any blood. All I see are ceiling tiles."

"They seemed to have come loose during the battle and have hit each person in the head knocking them out."

"Wow, that's an odd thing to happen."

Just then a squadron of policemen arrived and came into the conference room along with a medical team. Phillip Bartholomew, the Fire Chief also came in.

"Hey, what happened here? This is a complete violation of the fire code. The capacity for this room is only fifteen people."

"Yes, sorry about that chief."

"Let's get it cleaned up and move everyone out of here before something dangerous happens!"

"I think something dangerous already happened."

"Are you questioning me, boy?!!! Yelled the fire chief.

"No sir."

"Let's get moving then!"

Everyone involved in the shootout was eventually okay and was cleared to be released from the hospital. Dr. Delworth AKA Agent Hardinski/Agent Konevsberg somehow managed to elude the police and along with her accomplices, Luljet and Svetlana, were able to slip out of the hospital unnoticed. They had stolen some lab coats from three doctors whom they incapacitated and tied up in a nearby closet.

Snodgrass and Harper were investigated by the State Department but were cleared of any espionage charges. They were free to go back to their agency and continue their work as private investigators.

Wycliffe, Lars, and the Diwalis were all released and they each headed back to their respective countries.

Only Mr. Konevshenko was brought up on charges. He had an immediate trial and was sentenced to fifteen years in prison for espionage.

For Harper, his heart was broken. He had fallen for Luljet and believed he would never find a love like that ever again. Snodgrass tried to console him but it was going to take a while. In the meantime, he took him to the Whisby Falls part where they enjoyed the zip lines there. Although Snodgrass thought it would remind him of Albania and Luljet, it seemed to have the opposite effect and Harper was soon his old self.

Later on, at the City Hall, the boys were given the key to the city for their work in breaking up a spy ring. They got their pictures in the Whisby Gazette and became local heroes. Needless to say it was great publicity for the Snodgrass and Harper Detective Agency.

www.ingramcontent.com/pod-product-compliance
Lightning Source LLC
Chambersburg PA
CBHW070912100726
47907CB00008B/2297